What Not to Do When Summoning a Demon

Cover Artist: K.B. Barrett Designs

Editor: Dragon Smith Publishing LLC

ISBN-13: 978-1-961802-12-4

To everyone who's ever thought of summoning a demon to solve their problems.

And those who pushed me to finish this book.

CHAPTER ONE
CLARA

I never thought a jar of spaghetti sauce would be my downfall.

Yet here I am in a standoff with a lid choosing not to budge. At this point, it has to be intentional. If it wanted to open, it would.

The mason jar sits on the counter, mocking me. The old lady on the front is laughing at my struggle. Granted, she's always laughing since she's literally a label, but it feels personal. Especially since I have no idea who she is. My mother slapped her on the jars without ever explaining who the old woman was to our family. I should have asked when Mom made the stickers for her canned goods. I doubt context would make me feel better in this situation.

"Bitch," I mutter under my breath.

I've tried all the human ways to loosen it—the handle of a knife, hot water, a rubber gripper. I even borrowed a special can opener that's made for this purpose from a neighbor. It broke and now I need to buy a new one. I'm not exactly friends with said neighbor, and I'd hate for their impression of me to be borrowing shit I immediately break and never replace.

After all other tactics didn't work, I turned to the witchy ways. Not that I have a specific spell or potion to make this happen. Most of them revolve around intangible things. Opening a jar isn't exactly on the top of the list of spells to learn. In fact, I don't even know if it's possible. I could have gone out and bought some sauce and avoided all this, but it wouldn't have been the same. This particular jar is one of the remaining few from my mother's stores.

I press my lips together as my eyes alight on a book—*the* book. The one I shoved on the shelf above the counter next to my recipes as if it'll blend in and I'll forget about it. It's been handed down through the generations, from mother to daughter. I've read it many times, but I've never used any of the spells. Lessons on responsibility were drilled into me from a young age.

Being a witch wasn't something to take lightly. And the book was something beyond that. Until we had no other choice, we were to keep the spells unspoken. Until the need was dire, we were to leave it alone.

"This is a pretty dire situation," I whisper. Spaghetti might not seem that important to others. To me, my entire week hinges on whether I can open my jar.

Before I can talk myself out of it, I rush to the bookshelf and tug the book from the shelf. My palm brushes over the embossed cover. The dark leather seems to suck the light into it—a perpetual black hole. My mother's warning brushes against the corners of my mind. *Use with care, my dear. Everything with care. Except this—use these spells with caution.*

I close my eyes and drop the book on its spine. Usually, I wouldn't treat a book with such disdain, but this is the only way it'll work. Pages flutter through the air and I hold my breath. I glance down when they fall silent and scan the page.

"Demon summoning?"

My bottom lip ends up between my teeth. I suppose a demon would be strong enough to open a jar. I wouldn't have to ask them to do anything nefarious. Surely, there's an easier way to do this. A spell or potion, though I'd rather not melt the damn thing. I hem and haw as I bumble around the kitchen, making tea. My eyes keep darting to the book.

As I sip my drink from my favorite mug, I contemplate the consequences. Magic always has a price. Sometimes, it's small—a few minutes of sleep or a twinge in the shoulder. Other times...

Other times it's a massive payment—death.

Never your own life, though. No, because of course it's not. Such is the way when dealing with magic. I used to think it was unfair. Now that I'm older, I understand the need to maintain the balance in the world.

Sighing, I set my mug down and slam the book shut. When I turn, I come face to face with the jar. Pages flutter behind me again and I spin. The book is open to the demon summoning once more. I scowl, curling my hands into fists before I march over and slam it shut again, then shove it back into its place on the shelf. I'm halfway to my mug when I jump about a foot in the air at the thundering noise behind me. I already know it's fallen from its place and is taunting me.

"Fine," I snarl and grab the heavy tome.

I carry it into my spare room. It's supposed to be a guest room, but I turned it into my space for spell work. No use having a spare bed when I have no one visiting. Cauldrons, plants, and ingredients take over every available space. In the middle of the floor is an open area, and I set about drawing the summoning circle on the floor. It takes me longer than I want. I can't remember the last time I chalked anything on wood. I was never very adept at it. The moon shines through the window by the time I'm done.

Sitting back, I admire my handiwork. It's not perfect, but it'll do. Which is probably the worst attitude to have when summoning a damn demon. It'll hold them, though, and that's all that matters.

I pull the book toward me and finish setting out the various candles and ingredients I'll need not only to get them here but also to send them back. The last thing I need is a demon hanging around randomly.

When I'm done reading the instructions for the third time, I realize I'm stalling. I could walk right out of this room and finish my tea and go to bed. Except I'll be plagued with dreams and insomnia. They'll take turns harassing me throughout the night. And I really want spaghetti. I rush to the kitchen and grab the jar, then hurry back in.

Snapping my fingers, I light the red candles around the circle. I pull in a deep breath before reciting the incantation. I expected them to be in Latin, but it's literally just speaking with intention.

"From the depths of Hell, I summon thee," I say, my tone turning flippant toward the end, then press my lips together.

Nothing happens. The longer I wait, the more anxious I get. I've heard stories of other witches doing it wrong and the demon ends up in someone else's closet. Those tales never end well, but I thought they were fables to keep us from using the book. Now I'm wondering if I just set a demon loose on my quaint little town.

"Shit," I mutter as I heft the book in my arms and scan the page.

I did everything right as far as I can tell. I drop the book, no longer caring whether or not it's actually damaged. Maybe none of the spells work and this was merely a ploy from my mother. She was so serious when she talked about it. Doesn't mean she didn't have a wicked sense of humor. She's probably laughing at me from the grave.

Huffing, I grab the jar and make my way out of the room. As soon as I step into the hallway, the world goes dark and I freeze. What feels like an eternity later, the world rights itself and shadows wind their way around my legs. Slowly, I turn, all while trying to keep my breathing even as my heart attempts to burrow its way out of my chest.

"You summoned me...mortal?" The deep voice resonates in my body, making goosebumps explode across my skin.

When the smoke clears, I realize I may have fucked up. I've never seen a demon before. Sure, in pictures and shows, but

nothing could have prepared me for what they're really like. The tinge of red in his skin makes sense, yet the black swirls embedded in his flesh are not what I expected. He towers over me, though I'm average height, which also makes sense. Actually, he's more human than I expected, despite the black horns and silver hair. Asking about the three-piece suit would be a very bad idea.

"Not a mortal," he says with a tilt of his head. "Interesting."

"Uh, hi. I'm Clara." I fold my arms over the sauce. "And you are?"

"You want my name, witch? Is that your request?" He raises an eyebrow.

"Oh, uh, no. Can you...this may seem silly. Sorry." I step closer, holding out the jar. "Can you open this for me?"

I don't know if it's normal, but he looks baffled. Can demons be flabbergasted? I paste a tentative smile on my face and inch just a bit closer. I don't want to enter the circle with him. That would be disastrous. At least, I think it would be. If my arm merely passes the line, it should be fine. I hope it's fine because otherwise I won't be able to give him the jar to actually open.

"You want me to open the jar? You summoned me for *that*?"

I nod as he narrows his red eyes at me. When he blinks, they fade into a dull black. I really should have done more research on demons before I decided to summon one. This would have been a lot easier. Maybe I wouldn't be so scared. Or it might have freaked me out more.

"If you could, I would really appreciate it."

He tentatively reaches out and grasps the lid and I let go of the bottom. His large hands dwarf the jar and I wince. I open my mouth to plead with him not to break it, but I snap it shut when I remember who's standing in front of me.

His dark eyes meet mine and my stomach flips. I wrap my arms around my waist and sway while he studies me. It's like he thinks I'm tricking him. Honestly, if I was in his position, I'd think it was a prank too. Like, *hey, open this jar* and bam, a deadly

plague is released into the world. He's a demon, though, so maybe that's what he's hoping for.

With a quick flick of his wrist, the lid pops, and an excited giggle erupts from me. Hesitantly, he hands the jar back to me and I grin.

"Thank you. You have no idea how grateful I am."

He nods, wariness in his eyes. "You know you only get one request per summons, right?"

"Yup." I cradle the glass against my chest and glance up. "That's all I needed."

He crosses his arms and wings unfurl from his back, spreading to the edges of the circle. A soft *oh* falls from my lips and I force a smile to my face again.

"You have to say the words to release me," he huffs.

"Oh, that's right." I crouch and gingerly set the jar at my feet before scanning the text. "Um, I'm a little rusty on my Latin, but am I really saying 'begone demon' like I'm banishing you?"

"Yes. Or 'leave the demon' which has created more conflicts than necessary over the centuries. Just say it so I can get the hell out of here."

"Okay, then. *Discede daemonium*." I glance up and catch him rolling his eyes. It's such a human reaction I'm a little caught off guard.

As smoke swirls around his feet, his nostrils flare. "Your Latin needs work, as does your chalk work."

He disappears in a puff of smoke, the smell of sulfur and cinnamon lingering in the space. I grab my jar and turn to leave. What an absolute ass. My Latin is perfectly fine. I might concede on the chalk work, though.

"Well, fuck you too," I mutter. "And you used work twice in a sentence, asshole."

One of the shadows snaps out and whips me right in the ass. I yelp and glance over my shoulder. Two glowing red eyes stare at me from the dark cloud in the circle and I scowl. They wink out of existence along with the rest of the haze, though the warm

scent of cinnamon remains. Apparently he didn't like my parting comment much. To be fair, I probably wouldn't like it either, but he brought it upon himself.

At least now my jar is open and I won't be needing the book anymore. No more demon summoning in the middle of the night.

CHAPTER TWO
OMEN

The experience I had two nights ago is still running through my head. I keep waiting for the pull of a summoning again from the little witch. Surely she wanted more than just a jar opened. Except she was quite insistent. A smirk pulls at my lips as I remember her parting words. I wipe the expression from my face when I realize what I'm doing.

I'm sure the witch would be as confused by this room as I was by her chalking. It's surprising how human-like the space is, though the walls are made of obsidian. The long table and chairs were sourced during one of the many wars the mortals engaged in. None of us in my division were very happy when the witches called on us. Mostly because they were a disrespectful bunch. We weren't impressed. They haven't called on us en masse since. I'm more impressed my little witch was able to summon anyone, much less me. I'm high enough in the demon ranks not to be bothered.

I shake my head, wondering why I claimed her as my little witch. Calling her Clara seems...informal and personal. Neither of which we are to each other. I'm merely a demon who was forced to do her bidding.

"Omen, I need your latest report," Dimitri calls from across the room.

And now I have to write a damn report about it. "I'll get to it."

"Two mortal days is long enough. You don't want him coming down on your ass because you didn't do it." Dimitri says as he collapses into the chair next to me. They're ornate and dig into my back, but I keep sitting on them instead of smashing them into the walls.

"What's he going to do? Ground me?" I chuckle when he scowls. Dimitri's always been a stickler for the rules.

"Possible. Or send you down to level seven. No one wants that shit. You actually know what the hell you're doing."

"No pun intended," I mutter, and he scowls again. "If you keep making that face, it'll stick like that."

"What happened up top? Why are you putting it off?"

I grimace as I glance around. No one's close enough to overhear us. Doesn't mean I want to actually tell Dimitri about my little witch. *Not my little witch.* My encounter with *the* witch. If he spreads it around, I'll get even more shit about it. Humans, even of the witch variety, think we're petrifying. We are most of the time, though a lot of that is probably born from rumors. Demons are supposed to be unnerving and horrifying. Not that Clara seemed fazed by me.

"Okay, but if you say anything I'll set your room on fire," I grumble.

He smirks, raising an eyebrow. "Do go on."

"I was summoned by a witch." I clear my throat.

"Holy fucking shit. A witch? Haven't seen one of those...oh wait. Yes, I have. Because them and fucking teenagers are the only ones who summon us."

"Shut the fuck up and listen. She wanted me to open a jar."

He narrows his eyes, then glances around slowly. "I thought it was a box."

"What?" I pull back, searching my memories for a clue. "She isn't a descendent of Pandora. For fuck's sake. It was a jar of spaghetti sauce. Top was stuck, apparently."

His dark lips part as he processes what I've told him. I'll give him as long as he needs. I clearly didn't grasp the request at first. In my many centuries, I've never had one quite like it. Ludovic will certainly think I'm taking the piss out of him when I turn in my report. He doesn't have a sense of humor either. I'll be lucky if he doesn't send me back to earth to help Nex find errant souls evading him. It's tedious work and I fucking hate it. And I won't even be able to tell him no since he's technically above me.

"Was it good?" he finally asks.

"Was what good?"

"The spaghetti."

My jaw clenches. "I didn't stick around to eat it."

"Why the fuck not?" he cries, and I kick him in the ankle.

"Shut the fuck up. I opened the jar, then told her to send me back. She did." *After sassing me.*

He leans forward, propping his elbows on the table. "Well fuck. If they start asking us for easy shit like that, maybe Ludo will get off our asses."

I snort. "Doubt it. He's—"

"Got eyes everywhere. Write your damn report."

Dimitri shoves to his feet and prowls away, probably to terrorize some of the younger demons. A fresh crop came in a month ago and he's been spending most of his time dealing with them. Ludovic is supposed to be training them, but he foisted the job off on Dimitri. He wanted me to help, but I told him I was busy. I wasn't.

It takes me another ten minutes to start the report. As soon as I finish I vanish, aiming for my estate. It's not truly a mansion, but dimensions in Hell, like most things, are wonky. From the outside, I merely have a door. Inside is a maze of hallways leading off to a plethora of rooms. It's designed to disorient anyone who steps into my domain. I built it myself over several decades. There's even a lush bedroom—an oasis of my own. Contrary to popular belief, demons do sleep.

My clothes disappear, going to whatever pocket of time

they're from. As I collapse onto the silk bedsheets, I let out a sigh. I haven't slept since I was summoned. On earth it might be mere seconds between summoning and appearance, yet the journey is much more brutal from Hell. It's arduous and burns for some. Never for me, but it takes for-fucking-ever. Afterward, it takes a while for my body to settle. Exhaustion washes over me and darkness takes me quickly.

A yanking from my gut pulls me from sleep minutes later. I groan as magic swirls around me, forcing me between the worlds. Whoever the fuck got a hold of my summoning sigil is going to get my boot up their ass. Except I'm not wearing any boots. Or shoes. Or a stitch of clothing. I could fix my dilemma, but they deserve to see it all if they're bothering me while I'm sleeping. Not that they'd know.

Darkness wraps its tentacles around me, and I tense as the world shifts. The journey isn't taking as long this time. I wonder if the clothes slow me down or if it's a product of being topside just a short time ago. Either way, at least I won't have to swim my way through the inky night to get there. A loud pop echoes in my ears and my nostrils flare as a familiar room takes shape.

My little witch. I shake my head, banishing the thought.

Apprehension covers her round face, creating an adorable red glow on her cheeks. I squeeze my eyes shut, wondering where *that* came from. I doubt I've ever used the word adorable in my existence and I'm not about to start now. Just because she has a symmetrical face with wide blue eyes and glossy black hair and full lips doesn't mean anything. Although, now I really wish I grabbed pants before I got here.

"You again," I rumble, crossing my arms as I attempt to pull the shadows around my waist to hide my reaction to her.

"Me again," she says, framing her face with her hands. "Sorry, I realize you probably have other things to do, but I need another favor."

"It's not a favor if you summon me, witch." My nostrils flare

as her scent washes over me. Sage and lemon blossom—a cloying combination.

"While I'd usually agree, I need you to actually leave the circle. So, the favor is to actually come back when I ask instead of taking advantage of it. Which means I need something from you..." She bites her lip, a hopeful expression on her face.

"My name," I grumble, sighing.

I never used to have a problem with giving out my name. It's not like witches could do anything other than let me out of the circle. Unless they had my sigil, they wouldn't be able to summon me. She already has that, so my name wouldn't complicate things. My name is merely an insurance for her to send me back to Hell. I'm sure witches are taught something ludicrous, like they can brainwash us or force us to do their bidding. I could correct her, tell her it's not that serious, but what's the fun in that?

She twists her hands together. "I know it's probably a whole thing, but I promise I won't use it for anything nefarious. It's just my dad always said to have an exit plan that wasn't the front door. So, I feel like I'd be doing him a disserv—"

"It's Omen." I could pretend I offered it up because I didn't want to hear her talk anymore. I'm not ready to admit what the actual reason is.

She grins and picks up a thick, black book. "Well, my name is Clara."

"I'm aware."

Her smile widens. "Okay, Omen."

I grit my teeth, trying to ignore the curl of pleasure in my stomach. My name on her lips shouldn't affect me in any way. It doesn't. If I keep repeating it, my body might eventually accept it.

"So, now that I have your name. Omen," she says with a lilt to her voice. "I just need to find the spell that allows me to let you out of there."

"What exactly do you need me to do?" It's probably moving a box or something. As soon as I know, I can decide whether to tell her how to set me free instead of watching her thumb through the book.

"The batteries in the smoke detector are beeping. I tried to reach the thing, but it's too high even when I stand on the table. I wasn't about to put a stool on top of it. Tried that before and let me tell you, it was not a great idea. I swear I still have bruises." Grooves appear between her eyebrows as she studies the page, and I fight not to curl my lip at the book. "I figure you're so tall, you might be able to do it for me. You might have to use the chair, but that's okay."

"It's *daemonium dimittere me.* Although, just saying 'release my demon' might work."

She glances up, her eyes flicking to my cock, which twitches at the attention. Her tongue darts out to lick her bottom lip, further complicating the situation. Her cheeks redden again, and I glance away. It's been too long since I've bedded someone if I'm reacting to a damn witch. If she keeps it up, we'll be in a world of trouble.

I could summon my shadows, form some sort of shield around myself. I *should* do that, but I won't. The flush on her cheeks amuses me, along with the flash of desire in her eyes. Messing with her just might be the highlight of my night.

She speaks the words, her accent twisting the words in an unusual way. Slowly, I step out of the circle and she tenses. I slide into her space and tower over her. She presses her lips together, her scent morphing, and I smirk.

"Lead the way, little witch," I murmur.

She nods, then pivots, and her black hair brushes my chest. My palm itches to wrap the strands in my fist. She marches away and I follow. I don't know what I expected, but it wasn't plants covering almost every surface. The rooms in the cottage are small with ceilings much higher than I'm used to. I don't even have to duck under the doorways. She stops when we reach a tiny dining room with a table which only seats four.

"Don't make that face. It's a family heirloom," she snaps. Apparently the little witch has claws. I'm not surprised, though most witches fail to bring out their happy side when around demons.

"I wasn't making a face," I mutter as I use one of the chairs to hide my throbbing cock.

"Sure you weren't," she says under her breath. "Okay, so here's the batteries. That's the smoke detector. You know how to change it, right? I don't imagine it's very hard to figure out."

"I'll manage. Perhaps you should...get the fuck out."

She smirks, then flounces away. After a minute, things clatter in the kitchen, and I snatch up the batteries. I climb onto the chair, careful to protect my balls. I may be a demon, but it still hurts when I get knocked in the nuts.

The smoke detector is just out of reach, so I step onto the table. It takes me a minute to find the compartment and another two minutes before I figure out how to get the battery out. It doesn't look like the ones Clara gave me. My nostrils flare and I drop them at my feet.

"Witch," I bellow.

Her footsteps rush in and she squeaks, covering her eyes. "Sorry, uh, what's up?"

"These won't work. The battery is shaped differently," I grumble. I'd toss it at her, but she still has her hand over her eyes.

"What kind do you need?"

"How the fuck should I know? I'm a demon, not an electrician."

She shuffles forward, holding out her free hand. If she comes any closer, she'll be palming my shaft. "Just put it in my hand and I'll find it. Hopefully, I have one."

If she doesn't find one, I'm not sticking around. I drop the battery in her hand and she spins away to look, then rushes from the room once more. She'll have to summon me again if she really wants this done. Exhaustion pulls at my body. I wonder if I could curl up right here and take a nap while she's searching. It's been a while since I've slept topside. It's never as restful as I want it to be, though.

Clara skips back into the room, holding a battery up in triumph. She grins as she tosses it to me. I reach up and put it in, then close the little door.

"Do I need to press something to make it work?" I mumble.

She hums, then clears her throat. "You really have all the bells and whistles, huh?"

I glance at her and scowl. Her gaze is fixated on my cock. Actually, she's probably focused on the curved bars wrapped around my shaft.

"My eyes are up here, little witch," I growl, and her wide eyes flit to mine.

"I mean, if you didn't want me to stare, maybe you should have put on some pants."

"What would be the fun in that?" I smirk as she huffs and turns away.

I'm playing with fire. Good thing I'm practically made of flames.

CHAPTER THREE
CLARA

Omen's been on my mind more than he should be since he changed the batteries in my smoke detector. It's like he's infiltrated my thoughts and even my dreams. I blame it on the fact he popped in naked as a jaybird. Getting his physique and the extra metal he's sporting out of my brain hasn't been easy. It's annoying as shit.

Which is why it's his fault I'm halfway stuck behind my washing machine. I'm not actually stuck, but it still sucks. I was distracted when I took off my ring while doing laundry. If I didn't have Omen on my mind, I would have caught it before it rolled behind the washer. I didn't want to pull the machine out. Not that it would have helped since it's shoved against the wall in a small room.

I stretch, trying to gain an extra inch. My fingers brush against the metal and a screech leaves me. When I can't get it, I slam my fist into the washer with a yell.

"Fuck you. Dammit all to hell. Just give me a fucking break, please?"

I let out a choked sob as my chest heaves. I reach for it again, my muscles straining with the effort to reach my ring. An exasperated huff leaves me as the blood rushes to my head. I'm getting dizzy, but I refused to give up.

"Damn you, Omen," I whisper.

The edge of the machine digs into my stomach and I wiggle my body. If I go too far, I'll end up dying back here.

"Troubles, little witch?"

I jolt, smacking the back of my head against the wall. At least I didn't squeal like I usually do. I'm starting to think he enjoys jump-scaring me. I don't understand how he's here.

I wiggle again, trying to get out. The last thing I need is to have my ass in the air while a demon stands behind me. He's probably laughing at me. Or he's already left. Can he leave? I have no idea how any of this works. I really didn't think any of this through and I'm starting to wonder if I lost everything my mother taught me.

Magic has a price. Use the book with caution. Demons aren't friends. Witches stick together. Other than not making Omen my friend, I'm doing a bang-up job. If Omen keeps materializing without warning, I might be breaking that rule, too. Then again, he doesn't seem to want anything more than to do whatever I've summoned him for.

"While I'd love to sit here and watch you twerk your way out of this mess, I'm just going to..."

His hands wrap around my waist and his thumbs press into my ass. I let out a squeal, all my dignity coming out with it. I shouldn't care, but I do. For some reason, I want him to respect me. This is definitely not going to earn me a lick of admiration. I scoff as my palms slip against the washing machine. What I wouldn't give for one damn handhold. Actually, if I'm wishing for things, I wouldn't be in this position in the first place.

Omen picks me up and my head scrapes against the wall. An oof leaves me as my back hits his chest. At least he's clothed this time. His arms wrap around me and he swings around. Before I have a chance to protest, much less savor the pseudo hug, he drops me on my feet. I stumble and catch myself before I face-plant. By the time I turn, he's already leaning over the washing machine.

"This what you're looking for?" he asks, holding up my ring.

I snatch it out of his hand and scowl at it. "Thank you."

He grips my chin and forces my eyes to his. "It's customary to look someone in the eye when you thank them. And possibly not look like you're going to bite their head off."

A shiver rolls through me, though I attempt to suppress it. His nostrils flare and he steps back, releasing me. I swallow hard, unable to pull my gaze from his. His eyes flash red and he glances away, breaking our connection.

"Sorry," I whisper.

He clears his throat. "Why the fuck are you—never mind. What the hell is this thing?" He points at the washing machine.

"Uh, it's a washing machine. It cleans my clothes," I say, and he raises an eyebrow. "Wait. How do you know what twerking is, but not a washer?"

"Is a washer and a washing machine the same thing?"

I throw my hands up and spin around. I don't really know where I'm going or how to get rid of him. After he changed the batteries, he just sort of poofed out of existence. I assumed he could leave whenever he wanted. Throwing him out seems rude, but I'm in a pissy mood. I shouldn't take it out on him.

His footsteps follow me, and it takes everything in me not to confront him or even glance over my shoulder. I make my way to the living room and swallow a groan. I hurry forward and gather the clean laundry scattered on my couch. I spin around, my arms full of shirts, pants, and my unmentionables. His gaze dips down and I swear his nose twitches along with his lip. If he laughs at me, I'm going to lose it. I don't know what that looks like yet. Either I'll yell at him or burst into tears.

"Sorry. Uh, why are you here?"

"Because you were stuck behind a rinser machine."

I resist the urge to roll my eyes. "Washing machine or just washer. How do you know about twerking?"

"Dimi—another demon told me. He's not great at it, though he took great pleasure in showing me."

I nod, not entirely sure what to say. An image of Omen

bouncing his ass to a song with a heavy beat flashes through my head. There's no way he'd do something like that. He's much too grumpy for that.

"Did you try to do it?" The question slips out before I can stop myself.

He slowly shakes his head. "You're imagining me twerking, aren't you?"

"What? No." I spin around and drop my clothes on the couch. "Well, you saved me from a humiliating death. Thanks. Anything else?"

"Actually, yes."

I face him and plant my fists on my hips. "Let's hear it then."

He tilts his head. Fuck, I hate being mean. Even to a demon. Being confrontational isn't my style either. I'm more of a "bow out and pretend we grew apart" kind of person. Which doesn't even make sense since I'm rarely the one who leaves. Lately, my friends have been pulling away and I'm realizing I might be the throwaway friend.

"Well?" I prompt, then press my lips together.

He narrows his eyes. "Potato." He says it so seriously, I don't know how to react.

"Are you asking what potatoes are? Or do you want a potato? You're going to need to give me a little more."

"Dimi—someone said to bring back cooked potatoes since he knew I was coming topside."

"There a reason you—you know what? Never mind. Doesn't matter. What kind of potatoes?"

If he doesn't want to tell me about his life or his friends, that's perfectly fine. It's not like I'm going to share all my deep, dark secrets with him, either. It's annoying he won't even tell me his friend's name, which is clearly Dimitri.

He winces and moves his shoulders like he's shying away from pain. When he notices me watching him, his face goes blank.

"Potatoes are potatoes, aren't they?" he finally asks.

I pull in a deep breath, then blow it out slowly. "There are over four thousand different varieties of potatoes. Not to mention hundreds of different ways to cook all of the edible ones. So, technically potatoes are potatoes, but you're going to have to be more specific."

His mouth drops open, then snaps shut. It's such a human expression I almost laugh.

"Just name some things off and I'll tell you if it's right."

He glares at me as if *I've* done something wrong. I'm about to refuse when I remember I summoned him to open a jar of sauce for me. It's such a ridiculous request and he could have made things a lot harder than he did. Demons are known for fucking with those who summon them. At least that's what I've been told. Who knows if I was being fucked with or not when I summoned him? Certainly not me. Maybe that's why he just randomly showed up.

"This is ridiculous," I mumble, then sigh. "French fries, mashed potatoes, smashed potatoes, perogies, colcannon…"

He snaps his fingers and shadows swirl around his hand. "Fries. That's what he wanted. Do you have one?"

"Not on me. I might have some in the freezer." If he wasn't a demon and I wasn't a witch, this would probably be the weirdest conversation I've ever had.

I skirt around him and make my way through the dining room and to the kitchen. It's not until I'm rummaging around the freezer I realize he followed me. Once I find the bag, I straighten and begin prepping them for the oven. I avoid his eyes, though I can feel them tracking me around the kitchen.

"Did you know until recently it was illegal to carry more than fifty kilograms of potatoes in your car in Australia?" I peek at him from the corner of my eye and catch him shuddering. "Something wrong with the metric system?"

"Very funny, little witch. I'm not a fan of Australia."

"Why not?"

His face turns stony and I duck my head, focusing on spreading the fries out. The silence stretches on forever. I shouldn't have asked and I definitely should resist the urge to ramble, which is exactly what I did with the random fact about Australia. I've never even been there. He doesn't want to chitchat or be friends. He doesn't want to share witty anecdotes or gossip over tea. He's a demon. I'm a witch. This is merely business...over fries and spaghetti sauce.

The oven beeps and I slide the tray inside, my mind still arguing with itself over whether or not to fill the silence between us with inconsequential words.

"Spiders," he spits out.

I jolt at his outburst. I barely get my arm out of the way before the oven door slams shut. Tingles run up my hands and I heave out a heavy breath.

"Spiders?"

"They're not my favorite."

"Pretty sure every continent has spiders. Wait, does Hell not have spiders?"

I lean against the counter and finally look at him—really look at him. Past the horns and his silver hair. Beyond the red skin with the black tattoos. Are they tattoos? My body sways toward him, my fingers itching to trace them.

I shake my head and snap out of it. Why was I staring at him? Oh, yeah. It's because of the look in his dark eyes. The ones that occasionally flash reddish orange for no apparent reason. I can't quite place what emotion swims in their depths, but it's important. I can feel it in my bones.

His lips twitch. "First of all, spiders have too many legs. Second, we do not have spiders in Hell. The animals down there are...different."

I cross my arms. "Oh, I've seen the drawings."

"Witch drawings." He wrinkles his nose.

"I mean, there's some in the book." I point at the heavy soul-sucking tome back on the shelf next to my mom's recipe book.

The timer goes off and I set about dealing with the fries. Once I have them in a container, I set it in front of him. I don't know how he'll transport them or if they'll still be hot once they get there. His jaw twitches as he stares at the fries.

"Do you want dip?" I whisper.

"I don't know what dip is. I don't need it." He shoves to his feet and the stool wobbles. "Do you need anything else?"

I shake my head. I didn't summon him in the first place so I don't know what else I could possibly need. My new desk is being delivered soon, but I'm determined to put it together myself. I swore I would stop calling on Omen for things. Relying on him, a demon, will only end in disaster. He'll just end up leaving, too, and I'll be left to pick up the pieces of my shattered life alone.

He vanishes in a swirl of smoke, leaving only a whiff of sulfur and cinnamon behind.

CHAPTER FOUR
OMEN

I probably shouldn't have just poofed from Clara's house. She's clearly going through something based on her attitude. It was hard enough to let go of her when I fished her from behind the rinser—*washing*—machine. It took everything in me not to snatch her away when she almost burned herself. By the time she was leaning against the counter having a casual conversation, I knew I was in trouble. I had to get out of there before I did something drastic. Like throw her on the counter and bury my—

I suck in a sharp breath and blast into Dimitri's front room. I'm one of the few people he doesn't bar from entering his space. Usually I don't just waltz in like I own the place, but I'm in no mood to be nice. He's the reason I stuck around Clara's place. Him and his fucking fries.

He's nowhere to be found in the rest of the house. I shove open the door to his bedroom and find him sleeping. Fucker. I toss the container at his face, and he wakes with a string of curses.

"Special delivery," I growl, then spin to go back to my own place.

"Where the fuck have you been? And how are these things still warm?" he calls after me, and I turn in the doorway.

"I just came from topside. You said bring you fries next time. Now fucking thank me."

He stretches, his dark grey skin cracking open, revealing deep purple rivulets underneath. I wonder what Clara would think if she met Dimitri. After she stopped staring at him, he'd probably charm her within seventeen seconds. I scowl at the thought, vowing to keep them separate. Not that I'm going back to her place. I'll need to find a way to break the thread tying us together, which won't be easy.

"You've been gone for like three weeks. Ludo was about to send me after your ass. How long was it there?"

"Like an hour. Maybe." I scrub my hands down my face, suppressing a groan. I'm exhausted. Between dealing with things here and being summoned by Clara, I need a break. I'm going to end up crashing before long and there won't be anything I can do about it.

Dimitri pushes upright and leans against his headboard. "Triton wanted us to help with the gauntlet. I told him it'd have to wait until you got back."

"I'm not helping with the gauntlet. That shit is his area. It's his own damn fault he can't keep anyone around to work with the new demons coming in. Fucking asshole."

He pops off the top of the container and the smell of what I assume to be cooked fries wafts through the air. I can't deny they smell good. I've never had them, obviously. From what Clara said, they seem to be a staple in the human world. It wasn't even that I didn't know about potatoes. They've been around longer than me and I've been around forever, which gives me more opportunities to forget much of the things I've learned.

Sometimes I wonder what it would be like to have a finite life like humans. Even witches have the choice to extend their lives. If they tie themselves to a demon, they could technically live forever. Not that many take that option. Why I'm thinking about these things is beyond me. It's not like I want to keep Clara.

"Are you even listening?" Dimitri asks, cutting through my thoughts.

"Seeing as how you blather on more than Ludo, no. I'm not.

I'm going to sleep before I get sucked back into paperwork or summoned again."

He freezes, a fry halfway to his mouth. "You think your witch will pull you back? I thought she just needed the jar open?"

"And batteries changed in her smoke detector. And being saved from dying behind a human machine for soaking clothes. Next she's going to probably need me to clean the gutters."

"How the hell is it you know what a fucking battery and a gutter is, but you didn't know fries?"

I shrug and my chest tightens. "She said the same thing. Which is your fault, by the way."

"I asked for fries, didn't say where they needed to come from. It was your choice to ask your witchy girlfriend—"

"Enough," I snap. "That's not what I was talking about. You taught me what twerking was. *That* was your fault."

His eyes flash gold and a grin splits across his lips. "Tell me she twerked for you. No, no. Tell me *you* twerked."

"No one was twerking." Despite my protest, he doesn't look convinced. The image of Clara's legs wrapped in her tight pants, wiggling her ass in my face pops in my head. I swear I can still feel the softness of her flesh giving way under my grip.

"You want one of these? They're pretty good. Got a seasoning on them. Where's the dip?"

"What the fuck," I breathe. "I'm going to bed before I pass out."

He doesn't even look up from his potatoes, too busy doing a weird little jig as he eats. I could walk to my room, but I doubt I'd make it. I dissolve into my shadows and instant relief floods my muscles. I didn't realize how tightly I was wound until I release a little bit of magic. If I keep traveling between dimensions, my body will never regulate. Not only will time cease to exist for me, but I'll be consumed by my shadows. It's not a pretty way to go. Plus, I'll never truly be dead. Never at rest.

My room comes into view, and I slough off the excess energy trailing after me. I collapse onto my bed, letting out a groan. My thoughts empty and sleep licks at the corner of my mind. A tug in my navel yanks me awake. There's no floating through nothingness, no time to acclimate, no opportunity to adjust.

When Clara's bedroom materializes, my legs give out and I end up in a heap on the floor. My head swims and shadows billow around me. I don't have it in me to get up. I roll onto my back and stare at her ceiling. Patterns carved into the wood jump out at me and I count the swirls as I attempt to control my breathing.

A small ball of fluff lands on my chest, and sharp needles dig into my skin. A strangled cry leaves me as I bat it away. An annoyed meow echoes through the room and I groan, covering my face with my arm.

"A fucking cat?" I mumble.

"Omen? What are you doing here? And why are you on the floor?" Clara's voice soothes the jagged edges piercing into my head. Of course the cat ruins the moment by jumping on my chest once more. At least his claws stay sheathed this time.

"You summoned, little witch. You summon, I come."

She snorts and I smirk as I peek at her from between my fingers. My mouth goes dry as I take her in. Mostly she's been in shirts and pants—normal clothes other people probably wouldn't give a second glance. She's definitely not wearing anything like that now.

"What's with the dress?" I wheeze as she snatches the cat from me. The move puts her cleavage almost in my face. I lick my lips, then press them together.

She straightens, cuddling the cat. "Oh, aren't you just the most adorable thing. You're a good little kitty, aren't you? Handsome boy." She glances down at me. "Why are you on the floor?"

"Tripped over that damn cat." I didn't, but she doesn't need to know that.

I shove to my feet and the fluffball with a squished face hisses at me. Resisting the urge to hiss back at it, I pull in a deep breath. I'm not about to admit I'm on the brink of passing out. My body sways and I squeeze my eyes shut.

She huffs, and I glance at her. It's almost painful to see her with her hair in waves, pulled back from her painted face. She's both gorgeous and unfamiliar, which doesn't make sense. We don't know each other. We're not friends, lovers, or anything other than random beings who were thrown together.

"Oh, don't be mad at him. Kitty Cat probably didn't mean it, did you?" She buries her nose into his fur and the cat has the audacity to purr. Little fucker.

"Sure he didn't. Why the summons? I'm no good with hair."

She gives me a look, then sets the cat down. "I didn't summon you. It was just a slip of the tongue."

I could slip my tongue into—

I stop the thought before it can fully form. Between her innuendos and that dress, I'm sliding down a slippery slope. I clear my throat and glance away to survey her bedroom. It's less cluttered than the rest of her house. Whereas plants take up most of the shelves and windowsills in her living room and kitchen, not to mention her summoning room, there's no greenery in here.

Every surface is covered in notebooks and paperbacks. Sketches of flowers plaster the colorful walls, and a string of small lights hangs from the ceiling. There's even a fireplace set across from her four-poster bed. The grate's cold and I channel the emptiness before I face her once more.

"What was the slip?" I growl, keeping my gaze on her eyes.

"Oh, um, well…" She blushes and lets out a nervous laugh. "I mixed up Omen with…" She mumbles something I can't make out, and I raise an eyebrow. She clears her throat. "Brandon."

"Who the fuck is Brandon?" I blurt the question out before I can think better of it.

She laces her fingers together in front of her stomach. "Just someone I met at the coffee shop in town. He, uh, asked me out for coffee this afternoon. Actually, can you zip me up? I've been trying to reach it for the past ten minutes. Then my neighbor called and I got distracted."

The last thing I want to do is help her get dressed up for a

date. Not to mention I'll be incredibly close to her while I do it. I should walk away or disappear back to Hell. I could finally pass the fuck out. Once I get some sleep, I'll be able to purge her from my mind. She'll no longer haunt my dreams. She probably won't even summon me again.

Instead, I twirl my finger and a small smile flits across her lips. She turns slowly and I swallow hard at the strip of exposed skin. The fucking zipper almost reaches her ass. I should use my shadows, let them brush against her instead of my fingers. Then I'd only get an echo of sensation rather than my flesh on hers. With how tired I am, I doubt I'll be able to direct them. They'd go rogue and I'd have to deal with the consequences. Plus, the sensations will be so heightened right now, I'll have a hard time not throwing her on the bed—date be damned.

Gently, I grip the small piece of metal and tug it up. My knuckle skims across her flesh and goosebumps scatter in its wake. Her shoulders inch up, making it hard to pull the zipper all the way up. There's a small loop at the top and I brush aside a few stray hairs from her neck to hook the seams together. She glances back at me, swallowing hard while she forces a smile.

"Thank you," she breathes.

I nod, not trusting my voice. This is bad. Very fucking bad.

She steps away and I shudder. By the time she slips on her shoes, which are way too high, I've pulled my emotionless mask back on. I wouldn't fool Dimitri, but Clara doesn't seem to catch it. The cat winds its way around my legs, meowing incessantly, and I scowl at him.

She bends, giving me an ample view of her cleavage once more. My mouth waters and I squeeze my eyes shut. A stabbing pain lances through my head and I wince. My heartbeat hammers in my chest, drums in my ears, and threatens to suffocate me.

"Mr. Handsome, you're such a good little kitty." Clara's voice cuts through my panic and my breathing returns to normal. She doesn't even seem to have noticed I was on the brink of a magical meltdown.

"Why are you wearing that to a coffee shop?" I spit out, much harsher than I intended, and her head snaps up.

"Because I never get to wear dresses and this is one of the few I own. Now, I'm going to get going. Don't forget about Sunshine here."

She wiggles her fingers at me. Whether she's mocking me or being genuine, I don't know and I shouldn't care. The cat pads after her, then turns at the doorway and hisses. Fucking cats. I wonder if he can sense my emotions—the ones I haven't fully settled. Some familiars can do that, though I didn't realize Clara had one. This fluffball seemed to have shown up out of nowhere.

I sigh as the sound of the front door closing echoes through the house. It takes everything in me not to go after her and tell her to stay here. I don't. Mostly because I don't have a death wish. I don't need someone in my life, especially not a witch.

I need to shut down any thoughts of taking things further with her now before it gets out of hand. Before I can't resist her any longer. If I keep reminding myself, maybe I'll finally be free of this entanglement.

My head swims as I turn and call upon my magic to take me home. Shadows billow around me, casting me in a thick darkness. There's no pull in my stomach, no twisting of time, and no melding of dimensions. My eyes roll back and I can feel my body fall in slow motion. A softness engulfs me, and I have one thought before I pass out.

Fuck.

CHAPTER FIVE
CLARA

I had high hopes for this date with Brandon. I should have tempered my expectations. Going out with someone should be fun and carefree, at least for the first time. It shouldn't be weird. Except Brandon isn't making it easy.

He blabbers on across from me, his hands waving around. He's almost hit his coffee cup half a dozen times while he goes on and on about his fantasy football league. When he asked me if I knew what it was, I said I did, but apparently he heard, "tell me everything about it like I've been living in a cave for sixty years." It's annoying and I gave up trying to steer the conversation to something else. I stopped listening twenty minutes ago.

Now I'm wondering how the hell I can get out of this disaster. I don't have anyone to fake an emergency phone call with. My friends are still away on another group family vacation. I got the text about the trip right before Brandon approached me a few days ago. I blame my distraction on why I didn't notice the red flags waving in my face. Brandon was probably throwing them at me, and I missed every single one.

I'm loath to admit the other reason I jumped all over Brandon's offer to take me out. My thoughts have been entirely consumed with Omen and I need something to pull me out of this loop.

He's a demon. No matter how many times I remind myself of

that, I can't seem to stop. Thankfully, I've caught myself before I've summoned him again. I could have used his help to clean the gutters, which are still clogged. Or maybe help me with the vines covering the outside of my house. If I let them fester, they'll destroy my foundation, at least that's what the video I saw said. Doesn't mean he hasn't invaded every part of my brain, especially at night. I catch myself wondering what he's doing, if he's thinking about me, whether or not he wants me. It's unhealthy.

I've successfully kept Omen's name out of my mouth. Until today, and I didn't even mean to. My neighbor a mile down the road called about my package being delivered to her house. She asked what I was doing for the holiday. It took me a minute to figure out she was talking about the town festival, which is technically not a holiday. I don't even know why I was confessing anything to her. We're not friends, really. She keeps to herself mostly, enjoying her retirement. Before I knew it, though, she'd pulled the details from me and I accidentally said Omen's name. It was embarrassing even if she didn't understand.

"Have you heard of him?" Brandon's voice cuts through my thoughts and I tilt my head.

"Mhm." I nod, forcing a polite smile on my face. I feel like a bobblehead, but I'm liable to fall asleep if I don't move. "What do you do for work again?"

Annoyance flashes in his light eyes before he can hide it. "A club. Now, as I was saying—"

I tune him out again, making sure I nod and grunt every once in a while. My gaze wanders toward the barista behind the counter. Our eyes meet and she winces, then holds up a sign. I squint to make out the writing.

Need help?

I almost snort, then subtly shake my head. Her brows pull low and she rolls her eyes. At least I have one person waiting in the wings to save me if need be. Early on, I thought about just summoning Omen here. No one around here knows I'm a witch, though. Even if they did, I doubt a demon showing up in their midst would go over well. Besides, I don't need him coming in like a knight in shining armor. I straighten my shoulders, reminding myself I'm a strong, independent woman.

"He came into one of my clubs a few weeks ago. I'm sure you've never experienced something like that before. I could get you in if you'd like, though you'd have to wear something a bit... sexier." He smirks as if I'll agree with him. Besides the fact this black shift dress is the sexiest one I have, I'm not really the club type of girl.

Maybe he's just nervous and really, really bad at flirting. I pull in a deep breath, hoping I can salvage this. It doesn't matter if I never see Omen again. I may not have a future with a demon, but that doesn't mean I shouldn't have a future at all.

"You own a club? What's that like?"

He laughs a little too loud. "I'm the one who decides who's good enough to come into the club. Plus, I get free drinks."

"Oh, you're a bouncer?" Not that I care. Being a bouncer isn't something to be ashamed of, but Brandon seems like it's a great affront to his character.

He flushes, then puffs out his chest. "No, I'm a supervisor. Head Supervisor."

"Wow. That must be...a lot of work."

His eyes narrow as if he doesn't quite believe me. "I practically own the place. I just didn't want the responsibility of paperwork. Not that you'd understand that."

"Does that work?" I blurt out, and he gives me a confused look.

"Does what work?"

Fuck it. "Insulting women. I'm just wondering if that works. Do women swoon around you or fall into your bed more if you insult them? I'm genuinely curious."

"Listen, sweetie—"

"Not a great start," I mumble.

He continues on as if I didn't speak. "I know this might be hard for you to grasp, but I'm doing you a favor here. It's not an

insult to recognize one's shortcomings. And with the right partner, one can seek their full potential. If you let me fill in your empty spaces, the parts of your life you're lacking, then you can do the same for me."

"What areas are you lacking, Brandon?"

He gives me a disarming grin that makes my skin crawl. "I'm not great at dishes. Or laundry. See, those are the areas you could support me."

I set my cup down gently, resisting the urge to throw it in his face. I slip my wallet off the table. One of these days I'll learn my lesson. It's not often I go out. Every six months I get a bug up my butt, thinking I need something more in my life. I put myself out there and usually regret it. Actually, I always regret it. Doesn't matter who I meet, they all end up being duds or we don't mesh.

I should give up and resign myself to being alone. It would free me up for a fling with Omen if I had the guts. Which I don't. Omen is off-limits. If I keep reminding myself, maybe it'll finally sink in. Otherwise, I'll continue imagining him sinking into me. A flush travels down my body and settles between my legs.

"One last question, if you will," I say, leaning forward. "Who does your dishes now?"

"I eat out mostly, which I'm sure you'll appreciate once we get together."

I nod, pressing my lips together. "And your laundry? Or do you send out for that as well?"

He laughs, but there's a nervous tinge to it now. "I have someone to do that for me."

"Is that someone your mother?" I raise a single eyebrow as he sputters, and I huff out a laugh. "That's what I thought. We're clearly not compatible, Brandon. Thank you for the coffee."

I don't know why I'm thanking him. I bought my own cup when I got here since Brandon was ten minutes late. That's about the moment I should have left. Except I wasn't sure if Omen had actually gone back to Hell. The last thing I wanted to do was slink home in disgrace because I couldn't pick a decent guy to go out

with. I'm doing it now, but Omen is less likely to know about it. I can eat a pint of ice cream and mourn the loss of my dating life in peace.

"Wait, you're leaving? I think you're making a big mistake. Why don't you sit down and we can get on the same page?"

"I'd rather not. You're looking for a mother and I'm looking for a partner. It's perfectly fine to wait for someone who...meshes with you better."

I push to my feet and catch the barista's eye. She gives me a not-so-subtle thumbs up. Hopefully I won't have to drag her into this.

"No, no. You don't get to reject me. I reject you. That's how this works. Now, why don't we go someplace we can talk privately? I don't want you to get the wrong impression of me." He shoves his chair back and stands before reaching out for me.

Instinctively, I step back, almost tripping over my own chair. "No, thank you. I'm going home and so should you. Or go have a couple free drinks at your club."

Rage flashes across his face, twisting his lips. As quickly as it came, his expression dissolves into the affable one he had when we first met. If it wasn't for the barista behind the counter, I might be worried. He runs a hand through his light brown hair as he glances away.

"If you change your mind, you have my number," he mumbles, suddenly looking contrite. Part of me feels bad. Then I remember he tried to get me to hook up with him in exchange for me doing his laundry. I don't have the best track records with washers right now, so it's probably for the best.

"Have a good night," I say softly. I almost blurt out it was nice meeting him, but I catch myself at the last second. I make it a point not to lie if I can help it. If he turns into a misogynistic prick again, I'll do anything to get away from him.

I wave to the barista, then walk out the door without a backward glance. I'm kicking myself for not driving. Now I'll have to walk home, looking over my shoulder every few minutes.

Brandon probably won't come after me. If he does, well, I'll just have to hex him. I'm sure the book has something I could use if that doesn't work.

It takes me twice as long to get home with these heels, but I let out a sigh of relief when I turn onto my gravel road. Not the greatest footwear decision for this trek. I pick up the pace when my vine-covered cottage comes into view. My muscles relax and I lope up to the front door. With a protection spell in place, I feel a lot better about how I ended my date. The worst Brandon will be able to do is scream on my front lawn.

As soon as I'm inside, I kick off my shoes and struggle to reach the zipper on my dress. I can only get it a few inches down and I realize I might have to rip it to get it off. Summoning my demon —no, *the* demon—isn't an option. I have to stop seeing Omen as my backup plan.

My body flushes at the thought of him and I'm still trying to convince myself to forget about him when I stop short just inside my bedroom. My mouth drops open at Omen sprawled across my bed. I smother a chuckle with my hand when I spot his cat perched under his arm. He didn't strike me as a cat person. I make a note to ask what the cat's name is, since I can't keep calling him Handsome or Sunshine or Kitty Cat.

Omen looks different in his sleep. There's a softness to his features I haven't seen before. I wander closer until my shins brush against my comforter. Handsome stretches and yawns, blinking dark eyes in my direction. His squishy little face and his fluffy fur make me want to scoop him up and cuddle him. He'd make me feel better after my disaster of a date. He'd probably scratch the hell out of Brandon if I asked. I wonder if he's a hellcat. It would make sense.

I sigh, shaking my head. It's not like it matters. Omen will take the cat when he goes. From the way he was acting when he asked me for fries, he doesn't want to be here. He doesn't want me summoning him, and I need to respect that. Which means I definitely shouldn't touch him, no matter how much I want to.

Still, I reach out my fingers. A shout from outside has me yanking my hand back. Omen doesn't move, and I swallow hard before I spin around. I'm playing with fire. I slip from the room, wondering if I should wake him. There's more yelling from outside, though I can't make out the words. By the time I reach the living room and peek through the curtains, the noise has died down.

"Motherfucker," I whisper harshly.

Brandon, fists on his hips and face flushed beyond recognition, is screaming at my house. He must have followed me home. What an asshole. I squint, trying to figure out what he's saying. Something about owing him and demanding to be let in. I jerk back when he rushes the door. My protection spell will keep him out. He won't even get up the stairs.

Omen's cat winds around my leg and I yelp. Seconds later, Brandon attacks my door. Fear drenches me when the handle jiggles and I stumble back. My arms pinwheel as I fall over the coffee table. The cat yowls as it tangles with my feet, and I end up flipping over completely. Brandon hasn't given up, still pounding on the door.

I groan as my hair tumbles around me, free of the clip I trapped the strands in. As I push to my feet, my dress tears at the zipper and I wince. I glance over my shoulder, trying to gauge the damage. It's in no danger of falling off, so I leave it as I stomp toward the door.

Maybe my protection spell wore off or Brandon isn't quite what he seems. Doesn't matter since I'm going to send him packing. For all his bellyaching, I don't think he's going to hurt me. My protection spell failing is scarier, honestly. One man can't be that bad. By the time I reach the door, he's stopped. Something thumps against the door and soft sobs echo through the wood. I hesitate, then turn the knob.

Brandon's tear-streaked face and disheveled hair greet me. His gaze travels over my face, then dips to my chest before coming back to my face. Slowly, his eyes scan behind me, and I wonder if he's about to push into my house. I brace myself for him to attack. Despite how pathetic he looks, he could still hurt me. Alarm flashes across his face and he tucks his chin to his chest, then glances over my head and lets out a shuddering sigh.

"Something we can help you with, Brian?" Omen's deep voice rumbles through me, making me shiver, and Brandon swallows hard. "I didn't think so."

CHAPTER SIX
OMEN

I slam the door shut, then wrap my arm around Clara's waist. She doesn't fight me for once, just melts into my chest. I carry her back to her bedroom before I set her on her feet. Her shoulders slump when I step away. I can't trust myself to keep hold of her. And not for the usual reasons.

I don't know how her date went, but I can guess. I also don't know why I passed out on her bed instead of going back to Hell. Either way, I'm glad I'm still here. Clara would have ended up confronting him and who knows what that asshat would have done. Why she doesn't have protection spells on her house is beyond me. As far as I know, it's pretty common for witches.

"Stay here," I growl, then stomp from the room. Of course she doesn't listen.

My shadows snap out and shove her back on the bed. A string of curses falls from her lips and I smirk. They won't keep her there, but I have little control over them right now what with the rage rolling through me. My body still hasn't adjusted to time in this dimension. If I don't settle in one place for a while, I'll end up stuck. I don't know what would be worse, here or Hell. At least in Hell, I wouldn't be tempted to bed anyone.

I know the exact moment my shadows snap back into my body. Seconds later, Clara's footsteps scamper after me. My wings unfurl, hoping to keep her at bay. I'd rather not have her interfere

while I deal with Brandon. She'll try to step in and just get in the way.

I rip open the door to find Brandon collapsed on her front stoop. I glance over my shoulder. "Why don't you have a porch? Isn't that a witch thing?"

Her face does a weird thing. "A porch is not a witch thing. It's just...a thing people have?"

"All the witches I knew had porches," I mutter, turning back to Brandon.

"Is that so? And how many other witches have you had the pleasure of meeting?"

The corner of my mouth tips up as I slowly face her. "Jealous, little witch? Don't worry, it's a good look on you." My gaze drags down her body, then back to her eyes. "As is that dress."

"Are you flirting with me, sir, or dealing with the poor excuse for a date on my front stoop?"

I cross my arms and tilt my head. "Who says I can't do both?"

She sputters again, a lovely pink blush splashing across her cheeks. She presses her lips together and glares at me, then shoos me around. My nostrils flare as I pick up her scent. It's tinged with something I've never smelled before, though I can't place it. Shaking my head, I force myself to turn away from her and address the real problem. After I've dealt with the asshat, I'll go back to Hell and pretend I never started flirting with her.

"Well, Brandon, why are you still here?" I snap.

He pushes to his feet and throws his shoulders back. "Who are you? And why did you call her a witch?"

I step closer and he leans back, fear flashing in his watery eyes. "You come near her again and I'll drag you to Hell myself. Got it?"

I let the illusion I've masked my features with drop just enough for him to see my true form. He stumbles away and trips over his feet. I let out a chuckle as he spins, then sprints down the tree-lined lane. I turn and kick the door shut. Good fucking

riddance. What the fuck was she thinking going on a date with a man like that? I'm pretty sure he pissed himself before he ran.

"What'd you say to him? What'd you do?" She tugs one of the straps on her dress up, and I narrow my gaze.

"What's wrong with your dress?"

She rolls her eyes. "Nothing. I couldn't get the zipper down. Now answer the question."

"I just told him to leave."

She gives me a look. "He looked like he was about to shit his pants, which granted, he deserved, but still. What'd you do?"

I rub my jaw, wondering how much I should reveal. I don't want her thinking she should summon me every time she has a shitty date. At least, that's what I'm telling myself. The alternative is she means more to me than she should. I just need to get out of here. The sooner I get back to Hell, the better I'll feel. My nap, if you could call it that, wasn't nearly long enough.

"I showed him what you see. To a human, I'm sure it's a bit disconcerting. Why don't you have protection spells?"

"I do. Which is why I was surprised when he could knock on my door. If he had ill intent, he wouldn't be able to get within five feet. I don't know what happened."

"Perhaps he didn't have ill intent," I murmur.

"I mean, he probably didn't think he was being an asshole." She sighs and her eyes meet mine. "Will you help me get out of this dress?"

I grit my teeth and nod, not trusting my voice. She makes her way toward the bedroom and I follow, trying to keep my eyes off the small strip of skin she's managed to expose.

"What happened on your date?" I growl.

She waves her hand, dismissing my question. "Our...principles didn't align."

"What the fuck does that mean?"

"Well, I wanted to get to know him and he wanted someone to do his laundry."

"Why would you want—never mind." I shouldn't delve into her dating life or care whether she's seeing someone.

She gathers up her hair and lifts it off her neck as she presents her back to me. I yank the zipper down, but the fabric bunches. She shivers when my fingers touch her skin to hold the top, then tug on the zipper again. I drop my hands as soon as she's free. I should leave now. Except with the way her shoulders slump, I can't bring myself to.

"Do you want to talk about it?" I ask gruffly.

"No, I'm fine." She shuffles into the bathroom and pushes the door shut.

I don't know what I'm supposed to do. If she doesn't want to talk and I don't have anything else for me, then I should leave. My heart kicks up, pounding in my chest. I brace my hands on my knees and my shadows billow around me. I can't bring myself to go, especially without telling her first. The dark cloud dissipates and my pulse returns to normal.

Clara's cat streaks past me, his stubby legs working overtime. He blasts through the bathroom door and Clara flings herself around. If she wasn't half-naked, I'd laugh at the look on her surprised face. Instead, I slap my hand over my eyes. Swallowing hard, I try to erase the image of her without a shirt on. It doesn't work.

"Kitty, you can't do that," she scolds.

"Put on a shirt, little witch, or we're going to have more problems than the cat."

"Sorry to distract you, demon. Didn't think a human body would be such a big deal," she snaps.

"Only yours," I mutter as she slams the door, then raise my voice and call, "Why did Brandon follow you home?"

"Well, I was about to ask him that, but you threatened him before I could," she yells through the wood.

When she glides into the bedroom, my mouth waters. Gone is the tight black dress, replaced with a green t-shirt. I assume she has shorts on underneath, but all I can see are her shapely legs disappearing underneath the soft fabric. Her soft hair frames her face, no longer confined to a clip and pins. She's scrubbed the heavy makeup away, leaving pink spots on her cheeks.

She was gorgeous before, yet I prefer her like this. She's beautiful in an ethereal way. I swear she's glowing from within and I can't pull my eyes away from her. She smiles tentatively and glances down.

"Is there a stain on my shirt or something?"

I shake my head. "No. You look...fine."

Disappointment flashes in her eyes and I kick myself. None of this makes sense. Not her emotions or my reactions. I'm too tired to fight what I'm feeling. At least not tonight.

"Are you okay?" Clara asks tilting her head.

"Why wouldn't I be?"

She shrugs, glancing away. "Because I thought you'd be gone by the time I got home. Did you...did you stay to make sure I got home safe?"

"No. I've been bouncing between dimensions so often I'm off kilter. I wasn't able to get back to Hell."

I'm not about to admit I passed the fuck out on her bed. Then again, maybe I should. Otherwise, she'll think I did it on purpose. I open my mouth to confess when Handsome or Pretty Boy or whatever-the-hell his name is jumps at her. She snatches him up without hesitation.

"Look at you jumping so high," she coos, then glances at me. "I'm sorry about...well you know. I didn't realize...it won't happen again."

I have no idea what the fuck she's blathering on about. She could be talking about the cat tripping me or her disastrous date. Or summoning me in the first place. It may have only been a few days since she first called for me, but to her it's been weeks. Weeks of me popping in when she needs me. Weeks of her wondering if she should invite me into her space once more. Weeks of her living her life as if I don't exist.

"Omen, how do you know?" she asks softly, and my head snaps up.

"Know what?" The question comes out sharper than I intend, and she flinches the slightest bit. Regret douses the rest of my shadows, and they wink out of existence.

"I just meant, like time. How do you know how much time has passed if you're in Hell or here? Sorry, that didn't make sense. I mean, when you're here, how do you know how much time has passed in Hell? Does that make sense? You know what, never mind. It's not important. I'm just babbling now for no reason."

"Because you're worried about being alone?"

She winces and shakes her head. "I'm not. I doubt Brandon will come back. You took care of that. Thank you, by the way."

My spine straightens and I dig my nails into my palms. Clara thanks me too often. And apologizes too much. Witches don't thank demons. It's more than an expression of gratitude to them. It's a form of blessing and sacred. We demons aren't afforded those types of benedictions. If I remember right, such actions were punishable by...not death. That can't be right. It's been so long, I doubt Clara has even heard about it.

"Do you think you'll be able to get back home?" she asks, her voice wavering. She clears her throat and raises an eyebrow. I don't know what transformation she's gone through in those few seconds, but she's closed off her emotions completely.

"Won't know until I try."

I bow and my shadows whisk me away. I stumble as my feet slam into the marble floor of my bedroom.

"Why the fuck did I bow?" I mutter.

My vision wavers and I slam my eyes closed. I definitely shouldn't have traveled so soon. I wonder how much energy I expended by masking my true form in front of Brandon. Too much, clearly.

I collapse onto my bed, sending my clothes to another dimension. As exhausted as I am, I can't stop the images of Clara from marching their way through my head. One after another flashes in

my mind, faster and faster until my eyes fly open and I struggle to breathe.

If I don't stop this soon, I'll be consumed from the inside out. She'll destroy everything within me without ever realizing what she's done. Because of course she wouldn't. She isn't lying in bed pining after what could be. She's not going over every comment she's ever made to me. She isn't watching a slideshow of memories of my time there.

I'm alone in this torture, and the only way to stop it is to cut ties. I may not be able to stop her from summoning me, but I don't have to linger. No more conversations or touching her unnecessarily. I'll close myself off in every way I can. Eventually, she'll fade from my mind and I'll forget all about my little witch.

CHAPTER SEVEN
CLARA

I thought I'd be done with my demon by now. Summoning once was bad, even if I was desperate. Summoning him a second time might be worse. But a third time? I'm not counting the instances of accidental summoning. Those weren't intentional. Tonight, though? Tonight I'm playing with fire. Except I've been trying to put this desk together for the better part of the day. With the sun setting, I doubt I'll be able to finish it before midnight, if at all.

All my friends are out of town. They extended the vacation I wasn't invited to. Or maybe this one's new. They've pretty much abandoned the group chat. I don't blame them since it's a couple's trip, but it still stings.

Watching everyone else in my life move on to the next phase while I'm still here hurts. While I'm content with my life, sometimes I wish I had what they have. It was fine when we were all single. We shared our lives, our struggles, our triumphs with each other. They all have significant others to share with now, and I'm left with no one.

No one but my demon. Except he's not mine.

A demon who doesn't even want to stick around to talk. We're not friends and I'd do well to remember that. I'm pretty sure I'm not supposed to be consorting with demons anyway. Although Mom never said outright we shouldn't. It was more of an implied thing within the community. Mom just told me to be careful and think everything through. It was good advice, though I don't think I'm doing well at adhering to it.

Maybe I'm not content with my life after all.

I huff, throwing down the booklet. They're supposed to be easy directions to follow, but the print is too small and there's a hundred and seventeen steps and thirty-three bags of screws. Not to mention twenty-three individual pieces of wood. I'll never figure out how to put this desk together. I should have paid for the assembly. I couldn't justify paying an extra three hundred dollars when I'd already spent four hundred on the actual furniture.

"This is bullshit," I mutter, shoving the screwdriver away from me.

I wander into the kitchen and go through the motions of making dinner. It's way later than I wanted, which isn't going to stop me from making spaghetti. I'm still nursing the jar Omen opened for me.

As the scent fills the air, I'm transported to my childhood home. Closing my eyes, I breathe deeply as memories swirl through the air, weaving with the sharp tang of tomatoes and earthy scent of spices. It's just another sign of time passing.

My mother used to spend days with me at her feet while she canned the sauce. My father would waltz in with a basket over-flowing with vegetables, a grin plastered on his face. She never got around to teaching me how to do it and every time I've tried, something explodes.

When my dinner is ready, I post up at the island and pull the spell book closer to me. I've been taking my time to read through the whole thing again. I was obsessed when I was a teenager. Several pages are familiar, but I don't remember even half of it. Some of the spells are dark and twisted. I'd never use them regardless of how desperate I was. Nothing good can come from binding spells or severing emotions. On the other hand, I might use the protection spell for books. Regular protection ones are

great for my house, but one specifically for books? Yeah, I might use that one.

I scrape the bottom of the bowl for the remnants of the sauce. The book has a mind of its own and flips back to the demon summoning spell. The last thing I'm going to do is get Omen back here to put together a desk. I've already used him more than I planned. Eventually, I'll end up hailing someone other than him and it'll be...bad.

My mind wanders back to when Omen changed the batteries in the smoke detector. I tried to keep my eyes off his *very* naked body. I did not succeed. Who could blame me, though? I don't know if all demons are built like he is, but I'm not about to find out. I could search out another sigil, try my luck with someone else. Omen's wasn't even one I was searching for. It just sort of came out when I was doing the chalking. I still haven't washed the floor.

Resting my cheek in my hand, I twirl my fork. Omen's skin seemed to absorb the light, which only highlighted the silver rods caging his impressive cock. I'd like to say I didn't wonder what he looked like under the suit after the first time. I wonder if my thoughts became reality because of magic. Snorting, I drop my silverware into the bowl. As if I'm talented enough to influence the clothing choices of a demon.

"I bet you did it on purpose. Didn't you, Omen?" I laugh lightly to myself.

I focus on the book again and flip to the next page. Scanning the text, I wrinkle my nose. "Why would anyone want to brainwash someone?"

"Perhaps to control them, little witch."

I squeal, jumping up and knocking over my stool. Somehow the bowl ends up flying through the air and clatters across the island, coming to a stop right at the edge. Omen's hand snaps out and catches the fork before the tines sink into his face.

"Jumpy little thing, aren't you?" He smirks as I gape at him.

"What the hell are you doing here? I didn't summon you." I grab the book, though I don't know what the hell I'm looking for.

He snatches the tome from me and drops it on the island. "You used my name."

"But...but I...I *only* said your name. I didn't—" I wave my hands around as if that'll convey anything. "It's not like I actually summoned you."

He glances away, then back, his black eyes shining in the low light. "Do I really need to teach you everything? I assumed you were adequate at witchy things."

My blood boils and my stomach flips. Apparently, my face conveys just how much he fucked up. I'm so fucking sick of everyone telling me I'm not good enough merely because I don't flaunt my skills. It's why I moved away from my hometown. It was cliquey and toxic and tiny and witchy. Everyone there is a witch. And everyone competes with one another. They pushed me out long before I actually left. I didn't fit in with their way of life. They wanted to use their magic to make their lives better than everyone else's. They looked down on anyone who wasn't a witch. I don't even know why my parents decided to live there. Especially after it was clear I was a different type of witch than the others— quiet, easy-going, compassionate.

"I am a perfectly competent witch, thank you very much. Just because I don't know all the ins and outs of *demons*"—I spit the word out like a curse—"doesn't mean I'm not good enough."

Omen raises an eyebrow before resting his hand on his stomach and bowing slightly. "Apologies, Clara."

I didn't know what people meant when they said they were speechless, yet here I am. It's as if the words float just out of reach, tantalizing me with their succinct execution.

He smirks, raising a single eyebrow. "Did I break you?"

A shiver rolls down my spine, and I haul my mind out of the gutter before I blurt out something about his cock. "I didn't think demons...you know what? Never mind. Is there something you needed?"

"You didn't think we apologized? Of course we do. Though not often."

"Why not?" I avoid his eyes as I gather the bowl from the floor and search for my silverware.

"Because we rarely have anything to apologize for."

The fork appears in front of me, and I snatch it out of the air before scrambling to my feet. "How'd you do that?"

He shrugs, smirking at me. "Magic, little witch. Now why were you summoning me?"

I scowl as I round the island and wash out my dish. "Again, I didn't. So you can go back to wherever you were and do whatever it is demons do."

"Someone's in a bad mood," he murmurs in my ear.

Bastard seems to have done a one-eighty. He was curt and dismissive before. Even when he ran Brandon off, he acted like he didn't want to help me. The whole encounter was awkward and slightly humiliating.

I left for my date with such high hopes. Was I teasing Omen a little? Sure. He kept giving me mixed signals, though. He was snapping at me one minute and lusting after me the next. I'm not entirely great at reading people, especially demons, though. Just because I *thought* he wanted me, doesn't mean he actually does.

"I'm fine. Do you need me to send you back then? Or is there something you needed?" I turn around and lean against the counter. I expect him to be right behind me, but he's sitting on my vacated stool. How the hell did he get there? Doesn't matter.

"You realize time works differently in Hell, right? So, you summoning me after a week here was only a few hours in Hell."

"Well, it's been two weeks now, so how long has it been for you?" I cross my arms and my foot taps in time with my heartbeat. I'm not in a bad mood per se. I'm just annoyed at the desk. And at him randomly showing up. I'm embarrassed more than anything. I threw a damn fork at his head, for fuck's sake.

"About a week." His finger runs along the spine of the spell book and I swear it shudders.

"The math ain't mathing."

He smirks. "Of course not. It's Hell."

He glances over his shoulder and I scramble upright. I'd rather he not see the mess of parts sitting in the living room. I'm perfectly capable of putting together a desk by myself. There are directions and everything. Once I figure out which parts go with each picture, it should be a breeze.

"What do you do in Hell? Torture people?" I blurt out in a bid to pull his attention back to me. He swings around, his brows pulled low.

"What do witches do up here? Burn?"

My nostrils flare as I rein in the rage swirling between us. "You know damn well witches weren't burned. *Women* were burned. A witch wouldn't be caught in the first place. And I don't appreciate you making light of those events."

"Perhaps you'd do best not to make light of calling me a torturer, then."

Part of me wants to roll my eyes. The other is smart and likes my limbs attached to my body. We stare at each other, neither willing to fully back down. We're at an impasse, though I suppose he'll win no matter what. He *is* a demon, after all.

"I wasn't calling you a torturer. All I know about Hell is it's where bad people go," I murmur.

"What are you, six?" He shakes his head and mutters, "Bad people."

"Well, I forgot the word *evil*. Sue me."

His face scrunches up, and I swear he looks more human. "What does that mean?"

"Evil? How the hell do you not know the word evil? I'm pretty sure—"

"Sue. Is that a euphemism for fucking?"

I burst out laughing, tension sloughing off of me in waves. Which is exactly what I needed, apparently. I'd love to say I felt shitty because of the desk, but it's more than that. It's life drag-

ging me down. I was content until I summoned a demon. Which seems ridiculous.

I like my life and my house and my job. I don't have any family, but I have friends. *Used* to have friends. Until this moment, I didn't realize how much their absence impacted my mood. And how much I've been obsessing over it. The push and pull between wanting to be understanding and the loneliness at their absence has me all out of whack. Omen isn't the solution to my woes, though.

"It's...no. It's not fucking. It's...I don't even know how to describe it. Suing someone is taking them to court and getting money. It's just a phrase."

He scowls, his jaw clenching. "You humans and your clichés. Most of them don't make sense, anyway."

"They're clichés for a reason. Mostly because they're true."

I didn't think I'd be having a philosophical discussion about language tonight, but here we are. Then again, I never thought I'd have a conversation with a demon. At least he's clothed this time. This night would have gone a very different way if he wasn't. Not that a pair of pants and a t-shirt would stop me. I shake my head, dispelling the memories and the thoughts. Lusting after a demon is probably one of those cautions my mother was talking about.

"One in the hand is worth two in the bush? Doesn't make any damn sense and you can't convince me otherwise," he grumbles.

"That's a proverb. Not a cliché. Not that it matters. I'm sure you have sayings as well."

His fingers drum against the counter, his eyes taking on a distant look. After a minute, he snaps his fingers and grins. The smile transforms his entire face. He really needs to stop it or I'm going to end up lusting after him. Again. More than I already am. A little crush doesn't need to be acknowledged. It'll go away if he doesn't keep popping up. If I could just stop thinking about him and apparently saying his name, it might help.

"Every level has a fiery lining," he declares.

I tilt my head as my lips twitch. "Is that a joke?"

"Are you laughing?"

"No." I narrow my eyes.

"Don't you think you'd be laughing if it was a joke?"

I suck in my cheeks, wondering if I should tell him. "Pretty sure your little saying came from humans. Every cloud has a silver lining."

He's shaking his head before I've finished speaking. "You humans stole it from us. I'm confident."

We've veered wildly off-topic. He still hasn't said why he's hanging around. I may have accidentally summoned him, but he didn't need to stay. He could have poofed back to Hell as soon as he realized I didn't need him. Heat flashes in my stomach and cascades through my body to settle between my legs. Nope. Don't need him for that either.

"Are you avoiding something? Is that why you're sticking around?"

He glances away, refusing to meet my eyes. "Why would you think that?"

I smirk. *Gotcha.*

CHAPTER EIGHT
OMEN

I should have known my little witch would tease out my secrets. I suppose they're not really secrets. Granted, I doubt I would open up to anyone else about this. I just wanted a place I could go where nothing would be expected of me. If I have one more person dump a task on my plate, I'll riot.

I swore I'd stay away from her. Lingering, conversing, flirting —all on my list of things to avoid when it came to Clara. The moment she summoned me, all that went out the window. I'll break every vow I made while I tried to sleep. She's too... enchanting. She's somehow bewitched me and I need to figure out how to undo whatever spell she's cast on me. I had plans to tease it out of her, but tonight I just need a break.

"I didn't think demons just dropped by to chitchat," Clara says, pulling my eyes back to her.

"They don't. Although, they used to. Back when the world was...slower. We even had friendships with humans. Witches and demons often teamed up when certain events called for it." I brush invisible crumbs from the counter.

"Was there something you wanted to talk about?"

"Why are you in a shitty mood?" If I can keep the conversation focused on her, I won't have to talk about me.

She sighs, the sound filling the hole in my chest. "I was trying to put together a desk. It was...frustrating."

"What else," I demand. Because of course there's more. It's never just about one thing with humans, even witches. They stack their problems one on top of another until the first is no longer visible. They may strip off a few layers and deal with those, yet they never get to the root of anything.

"Why can't it just be the desk?" she snaps. She leans over the counter and snatches up the spell book.

She stalks around the island, clutching the tome to her chest. She disappears into the dining room, and I take a deep breath before following her. Leaning against the wall, I watch her grumble under her breath as she drops the book onto the table and picks up what looks like an instruction manual. I'm not about to interrupt her, lest I get snapped at again.

"Perhaps I'm not the only one avoiding things," I mutter.

"And what are *you* avoiding?"

"Paperwork, mostly."

She glances up, her nose wrinkling and her lips twitch. It's adorable and I have to look away before I comment on it. She's distracting in a way I'm not used to. She may be a witch, but she's also a human. I have to remind myself not to woo her, bed her, and keep her. No matter how adorable she is, she's still a witch who would take too much of my time. Then again, she's already doing that even when she's not summoning me. I shake my head, focusing on my current plan—hiding.

She sweeps her dark hair over her shoulder, making me imagine the strands wrapped in my fist. "Demons have paperwork?"

"And upper level demons. I believe you call them managers here. They're just as annoying down there, always nitpicking their way through things. You didn't exactly help anything, either."

She tips her head back. "It was the jar, wasn't it? I'm sorry."

"Not your fault. You merely wanted it opened. It was the easiest summoning I've had in decades," I say with a chuckle.

"You've had easier ones?" She wraps her arms around her legs and rests her chin on her knees.

My back itches, an ache settling between my shoulder blades. Hiding my shadows for so long hurts, but usually not this quickly. I'll have to release some of this pent-up energy soon. The easiest way would be to form wings. Except that would make me hot, which would then require me to take off my shirt and I don't know if I want to spend the rest of the night half naked. Especially with how her eyes keep darting to my crotch. It's been weeks since she saw me naked. Maybe she's been checking me out every time I've been here since and I didn't notice. I was too busy trying to ignore the pull toward her.

"I had a witch ask to me to gather herbs for him in the forest. No one would go into the trees because of some ancient lore. They said the trees rose up, attacking their ancestors and the woods had birthed some terrifying creature."

"What kind of creature?" she whispers.

I fight a grin. "I never saw it. They said it would devour their ancestors whole. I thought it was ridiculous."

"Of course you did," she mutters, but I can tell she's fighting a smirk. "You don't seem one prone to whimsy or fairytales."

"You'd be surprised, little witch. Anyway, turns out they were right."

Her eyes widen. "What was in there?"

"There was a very large clearing in the middle. In the dead of night, something would nest there, making an awful racket." I fight back a smile as she hangs on my every word. "When I got there, I found a herd of...elk."

She scowls, shaking her head. "That's not funny."

"It was a little funny. Of course, they didn't believe me until I sent the elk running out of the forest."

She presses her lips together and focuses on the instructions again. "Well, that seems like quite a bit more work than opening a jar."

"What's your issue?"

"Nothing. I'm just feeling sorry for myself." She gathers some of the tools closer, using the directions to avoid my gaze.

A twinge hits my muscles and I wince. I give up and pull my shirt over my head. Clara squawks, but I ignore her as I unfurl my wings with a sigh of relief. Stretching the talons on each tip helps ease the last bit of ache. Smoke fills the room, wrapping me in a warm blanket of comfort. Spending so much time topside still drains me. I thought after my nap and some time in Hell, things would be easier. Apparently not.

"Uh, don't knock my pictures off the wall," she says.

I glance to my left and find the frames she's talking about. Several humans gathered around a fire, their smiling faces shining with joy. I always envied humans and their ability to capture these moments. There are no pictures in Hell.

"Are these your friends?"

"Yeah. Most of them are married or have moved away. They're on another weekend getaway right now. Taking advantage of the weather and all that."

Given the look on her face, that's what's bothering her. I could tease out the reasons behind it all, but I doubt she'd open up. Delving deeper into her life might help me find the thread connecting us, though. Clearly, the universe has plans for us. Or this could be someone fucking with me, making me believe we're linked together for some other purpose when we're really not. Getting Clara to talk would reveal a lot. Demons aren't what one would describe as good listeners, especially when it comes to witches.

She mutters under her breath, picking up various pieces of wood and slamming them back down. It's painful to watch her struggle.

When I can't take it anymore, I prowl to her. Sliding my hands under her arms, I lift her up as she squeals. I set her down several feet away and quickly drop my hands. I didn't think through any of my actions and now I'm paying the consequences as I ease into her vacated spot on the floor. My cock protests, straining against my pants. My hands tremble and I swallow hard. I keep touching her and every time it backfires on me.

"Go make tea," I growl while she gawks at me.

I pick up the instructions and squint at the tiny print. After she walks away, cussing me out as she goes, I toss them aside. They're indecipherable. Whoever wrote them clearly had no idea how to put a desk together. It takes me at least another five minutes to figure out which part is the leg and which is the top. My frustration grows with each passing second.

Clara sets down a mug next to me, the sweet aroma filling the air, and I grunt. I've forgotten most of the customs of witches, but demons don't thank them. Clara doesn't seem to care, though, as she sinks onto the couch with her own mug.

"Where the hell does this piece go?" I mutter more to myself than anything.

"Now do you understand why I was frustrated?"

"If you're going to make snide comments, go away." I wave my hand at her before attempting to open a bag of tiny screws. They're probably not small for the little witch, but my fingers are much larger than hers. I can span her waist—hell, her hips—with both of mine. My wings quiver with the reminder and I struggle to get my shit together. This was a very bad idea.

"Would you like some help?"

I grit my teeth. "No."

"You must really hate paperwork if you're willing to put a desk together without me asking," she says behind the rim of her mug. Her eyes twinkle as she takes a sip.

"I'm missing a meeting as well. Does that help ease your mind?" The tool slips from my grasp as I attempt to fit everything together.

She hums and I work in silence until she clears her throat. "What's the meeting about?"

"Something about the veil thinning. It happens every year. I don't know why they feel the need to gather everyone and talk about it. The instructions don't change. I swear I've been to three thousand meetings and they all say the same thing."

"Could've been an email, huh?" She laughs lightly, and I glance up at her.

"What's email?"

She shakes her head, a smile playing on her lips. "It's like a note."

When her tongue darts out to lick the bottom one, I tuck my chin to my chest. I really need to get laid. Preferably with someone who doesn't summon me every five seconds. If I sleep with my —*the* little witch, it'll end up being awkward. Unless I gave her another sigil so she could summon some other demon. The thought sends flames licking at my fingertips and I drop the piece of wood I'm holding.

"Shit, are you okay?" Clara rushes toward me, her hands hovering over my skin.

Her shoulder brushes my wing and I jolt. Dimitri won't stop expounding on how much he loves when someone touches his wings. I am nothing like him. He uses that knowledge against me more often than I'd like. Clara touching me is nothing like him. What does it say about me that a mere skim of her flesh against my wings has my cock hardening? The shadows that make up my wings may be rooted in magic, but they're not as sensitive as my actual skin. I'm sure if they were actual wings, I'd be bending her over the couch and having my way with her.

"I'm fine," I grunt. "I'm practically made of fire, Clara." Her name rolls off my tongue with ease.

"Guess they wouldn't be able to burn you at the stake, huh?"

"Was that a joke, little witch?"

She snorts, settling across from me on the floor. "Did you laugh?"

"Touché. You know, there were witches burned at the stake. Just not by humans."

"Excuse me?"

I shrug, not really wanting to give her a history lesson about her own people. I pick up one of the many tools she was using. Why she'd need a hammer when these are all screws is beyond me.

Clara huffs and rips it from my hands. "Explain."

"Some witches got out of control. Their heads got a little too far up their asses, and they started dabbling in some shit they shouldn't have."

She purses her lips, narrowing her eyes. "So, demons...burned them?"

I shrug again, wishing I would have kept my damn mouth shut. "It was necessary."

"How the hell is that necessary?"

"Clara, not all witches are like you or the witches you grew up with. They were rotten to the core and infecting others. Remember that mind control spell? That's where they began and it only got worse from there."

Deep grooves appear between her eyes. It's hard to fully explain the extent of their corruption, especially to someone like Clara. I don't know a lot about where she grew up, but I know a little. Dimitri was kind enough to find out more about her and keeps slipping me tidbits of information. I'd be pissed, except he needs a side quest to occupy his time. If he keeps calling her my witchy girlfriend, though, I might stab him.

"You can give up on the desk. I'll deal with it tomorrow," she murmurs.

I don't want to go back. It's more than just the meeting and the paperwork. I was content for several decades. Even recently, I didn't need more than what I was doing. Training demons as they move up the ranks, traveling to different dimensions of Hell, and even running errands—it filled my time at the very least. Lately, I'm struggling. I'd rather spend my time here putting together a desk and pretending it has nothing to do with the witch sitting across from me.

"Why do you need a desk?" I ask, fitting another screw in a hole that's much too big.

"I sell plants. It comes with its own paperwork, and my back hurts when I work on it in bed or on the couch."

"You have a business?"

"Yes...why?" Her lip slips between her teeth, and I have the irrational urge to bite the plump flesh.

I shake my head, wishing I would have kept my damn shirt on. "No reason. Just wondering."

A jingle rings through the space and I glance around. She jumps up and strides from the room. I have no idea where the music came from or what she's doing. Instead, I focus on the parts in front of me. It's the only way I'll be able to ignore whatever's happening between us. None of this makes any fucking sense—with Clara or with the desk. I pick up one piece of wood after another and throw it down again. It doesn't matter how I fit them together, none of it works. My frustration grows with each second until smoke rises from my skin.

"Fuck this," I mutter.

I snap my fingers and the pieces fly into place. It's so quick, I can barely follow them fitting together. Shadows swirl around the desk and I smirk. None of the screws were used, but that shouldn't matter.

"You're telling me you could do that this whole fucking time? You asshole," Clara cries from the doorway.

She stomps toward the desk and runs her hand along the top. She brushes a finger along the burn mark I left behind. If she complains about it after I saved her all that time and frustration, I might lose it on her. Then again, bantering with her has been... fun. Exhilarating even.

She huffs, pulling me from my thoughts, and she drops onto the couch. I didn't even notice the basket full of clothes. As she starts folding them, I wonder if this is her polite dismissal. I don't know how long it's been in Hell, but I doubt the meeting is over. And the paperwork will still be waiting.

"Thank you for putting the desk together." She unfurls a towel and hides behind it. "Am I annoying you?"

"What? Why would I be annoyed?"

She sighs as she drops the fabric and levels me with a stare. "Because I keep summoning you and making you do all these tasks for me. Seems to me as a demon, you'd have better things to do. Plus, all I've ever done for you is make you fries. And those weren't even for you."

I lean back on my hands. "You're not annoying, Clara. Now, tell me about this vacation."

CHAPTER NINE
CLARA

My eyes flutter open, and I stare at the ceiling for a bit before I figure out where I am. Lumps from the old couch dig into my back and I groan. Turning on my side, I narrowly avoid dumping myself onto the floor. My hand flops around and I almost smack myself in the face.

"What the hell?" I groan as I push upright.

I almost feel like I got drunk last night and am paying for it now. I didn't. At least, I'm pretty sure I didn't. My memories slowly return as I massage my fingers. Omen was here. I accidentally summoned him, yet he stuck around. It must have been a dream, though. Otherwise, it'd mean he was here. And I opened up to him about my feelings.

No, it must have been a dream. Why would a demon hang out? Especially with a witch. It doesn't happen as far as I know. Most witches aren't summoning demons in the first place.

My eyes catch on the desk, decidedly not in pieces and sitting in the middle of the living room. I scramble to my feet, then slow, brushing my fingers across the burn marks gracing the top. I had plans to paint it, but I don't know if I'd be able to now. Having Omen here, drinking tea and bitching over a desk, was refreshing. I don't have it in me to resent my friends, but having no one to talk to hasn't been easy.

When he asked about the vacation, I tried to play it off as no big deal. They're free to do whatever they want. Not even getting an invitation, though...hurt. Thank fuck I didn't start crying in front of him. It was embarrassing enough to spill my guts. Tears would've made it worse. Other than paperwork and meetings, he didn't really tell me anything. I wonder if he's even allowed to.

"Hopefully, he doesn't get in trouble," I mutter.

Even though he didn't open up about his deepest, darkest secrets, he revealed a lot more than I expected. He told me about his place in Hell and what happens when I summon him. Between him explaining pocket dimensions and the shadows always swirling around him, I feel like I got a glimpse of the demon underneath the reddish skin and horns.

I'm sure he just had no other place to go, but a thrill rolls through me that he stayed with me. Which is exactly what I *shouldn't* be feeling. Reminding myself he's a demon I should stay away from gets harder and harder with every interaction.

I hum to myself as I make my way to the bathroom. Am I fantasizing about what it would be like if he were here more often? Maybe. Do I realize it's futile? Absolutely. Still, a witch can dream. Especially since I know what he looks like naked.

I go about my normal routine of showering, dressing, and throwing my hair up in a ponytail. I play our conversation from last night over and over in my head. By the time I start making breakfast, I'm lagging. The singing has stopped and my mind is mush.

Sleeping on the couch was not smart. I'm surprised I didn't fall off in the middle of the night. I glance at the clock in the kitchen, wondering what time he left, and realize I slept through breakfast and most of lunch. I'm not hungry, but I shouldn't waste the food.

There's a nervous energy permeating the space—the entire house, really. I end up in my bedroom, stripping down to just a tank top and underwear. Flicking the heavy curtains over the windows, I'm plunged into darkness. As I slide between the cool sheets, my eyes grow heavy. I haven't even been up for more than

an hour, but my body is clearly done for the day. A nap will help clear the current of electricity swirling about. If I had it in me, I'd brew some herbs to cleanse everything. Except it doesn't feel malevolent. It's just *different.* I wouldn't be surprised if Omen was the cause. I wouldn't know since I've never entertained demons before.

My muscles relax one by one and I close my eyes, waiting for sleep to take me. It doesn't. Because she's a fickle bitch. I doze for I don't know how long, flipping from one side to the other. I end up staring at the dark wood above me after a while. My mind wanders back to Omen. More specifically to the cage piercing his cock.

A giggle slips out, and I'm pretty sure I'm blushing. A jittery energy washes over me, which is probably because I haven't been laid in forever. I gave up on one-night stands long ago. There aren't many single people in my small town and I haven't had much luck with dating apps, as evidenced by my last encounter. No one wants to travel an hour for a first date, myself included. Brandon was a fluke—a last-ditch effort to see if I could find someone and stop fantasizing about a demon.

Still, it's one thing to admire Omen's body and completely another to imagine what it'd be like to sleep with him. It's not like he's here, though. He'd never know I was getting off to my memories of him. And it's his fault, anyway, what with his flirtatious innuendos and that devastating smirk. He knows exactly what he's doing. Besides, I need something to help my body relax and this is the easiest solution at my fingertips. Literally.

I scratch my nails across my sheets, debating whether I should pull out my toy or get up and be productive. The toy wins, and I fish it from my nightstand.

When I close my eyes, an image of Omen decked out in a whole lot of nothing flashes behind my lids. A shudder runs through me as I slip off my sweatpants and underwear. I debate taking off my tank top, then decide against it. I slide one hand under the fabric to cup my breast and the other between my legs.

Fantasy Omen's lips twitch at how wet I am. It's hard to pretend it's him touching me instead of my own hands. I bet his long fingers would have my body in a puddle at his feet. At this point, all he'd have to do is give me a come-hither smirk and I'd be running. Which I will blame solely on my dry spell and not on the fact he seems to know exactly how to seduce a woman—witch or not.

Huffing, I focus on the pleasure building in me. Heat flashes through my body as I pinch my nipple. I grab the vibrator and press the button, but nothing happens. I flip back the covers and push harder until a buzz fills the room. At the first touch, I jolt and squeeze the toy. It changes the setting, going from a constant purr to a rhythm I know no one uses. Who wants to be hit with a bolt of pleasure every three point seven seconds? I end up cycling through all the modes before it starts over.

I let out a sigh and close my eyes again. For something that's supposed to be exhilarating, it's becoming more hassle than it's worth. A soft moan leaves me when I find the right spot. My knees fall open and the comforter slips to my feet. Euphoria fills me up, one drop at a time. Part of me wishes I would have grabbed the other toy so I have something to clamp down on, but I'm not about to stop now.

Just as I'm about to tip over the edge, the toy stops. I press harder into my clit, waiting for it to start up again. A little more and I'll finally have relief. Omen's voice whispers in my ear, goading me on. With a groan, I use the now-silent vibrator to circle the sensitive spot. My legs shake as my orgasm sits just out of reach. A strangled cry leaves me as the vibrator explodes to life.

I suck in a sharp breath, squeezing my eyes shut as I scramble to seize my only chance at a climax. I don't know why I'm still trying. Giving up would be easier. Hell, calling for Omen to help me out would be the best solution. And the worst. He probably hasn't touched himself to thoughts of me. A random witch who summoned him? Not exactly a master seductress.

My palm slides from one breast to the other, imagining the

fingers are someone else's. A particular someone. I squirm as memories of him and his special hardware flit through my mind. I dance on the edge, desperately trying to hurtle myself into oblivion. My pussy spasms once, then twice.

Frustration hits me and I huff, dropping the toy between my legs. It's probably because I stayed up half the night. Or I'm just *too* horny. I don't know if that's a thing or not, but I wouldn't be surprised. Blaming Omen probably isn't fair. I'm going to do it, anyway.

"Need some help there, little witch?" Omen's deep timbre flows over me and my eyes flutter closed.

Then it hits me. His voice wasn't in my head.

I shriek, rolling as I tug the comforter over my naked body. I keep moving until I fall over the side of the bed. Strong hands grab me and lift me up. I bury my burning face in the covers.

"How long were you standing there?" I moan, curling in on myself.

He chuckles as he sits on my bed and settles me on his lap. "You *did* call me, Clara. You should have known I'd show up once you summoned me."

"So you just hung around watching while I...while I..." I scrunch up my nose, unable to finish.

I'm not a prude or anything. Talking about sex isn't something I shy away from. Except I've never been in this particular position before. No one's ever caught me in the act. Especially while moaning their name.

"While you played with your pretty—"

I shriek again and struggle to slap my hand over his mouth. Except I'm bundled up in a blanket and I can't see him. His booming laugh rumbles through the air, sending a shiver through me. He barely cracked a smile last night, though he was more relaxed than I'd seen him before.

"Can we just pretend this didn't happen? And can you put me down?" I mumble through the fabric.

Without a word, he sets me gently on the bed. The mattress

dips as he stands. By the time I extricate myself from the covers, he's gone. I glance around the room, wondering if he'll pop back up. As the silence stretches, I realize he actually left.

"That's not what I meant," I yell.

No one answers.

CHAPTER TEN
OMEN

Dimitri collapses next to me, sweat dripping down his body. My nose wrinkles, though I'm not much better. Neither of us talk as we watch a lower-level demon run the gauntlet. We usually don't have to participate in these things, but Triton thought it would be good for the younger ones to see us. I didn't complain until he made us do it again and again.

"How's your witch?" he says finally, and I glare at him.

"Not mine. And keep you fucking voice down." The last thing I need is someone overhearing and ratting me out to Ludo. I've been fudging my reports, making it seem like I'm going topside for other things. Admitting I've been summoned by Clara half a dozen times isn't something I want to do.

Dimitri rolls his eyes and swipes a hand over his face. "So?"

"Haven't seen her."

An image of her the last time I did pops into my mind. I grit my teeth and shove it away. It's not like I was there very long while she played with herself. Long enough for the picture to implant in my brain and replay while I slept. I've woken up too many times with my cock in my hand while the echo of her moans rings in my ears. It's too much and not enough. And definitely not something I should act on.

Waltzing into her house and fucking her how she deserves to be fucked should not be at the top of my fantasies. She's a human.

Not to mention a witch. The argument becomes flimsier the more I repeat it. One of these days, it'll crumble entirely and nothing will stop me from showing up without being summoned.

"You piss her off? You know how volatile they can be." He laughs as if he's dropped the funniest joke this century.

"She's not like that," I mutter, immediately wishing I would have kept my mouth shut.

He turns wide eyes to me, a grin plastered on his face. "Oh, she's not? Well, I stand corrected. Perhaps we should have a little meet up and—"

"Don't even fucking think about it. Stay away from her. It's bad enough I'm going there. She doesn't need a whole host prancing through her fucking kitchen," I growl.

He brings his hand to his chest and gasps. "I do *not* prance. I am as graceful as a—"

"Dimitri," Triton bellows. "Get over here and demonstrate how to not get sawed in half."

He jumps to his feet and rushes over. Triton motions for me to follow, and I chuckle under my breath. He scowls before turning his attention to Dimitri. My friend can't say no. It's bred into him to follow orders. I don't know what went wrong with me, but I never had issues making my own decisions. It caused a lot of problems when I was younger. I've been around long enough now, no one fucks with me.

Except Clara.

I shake my head and push to my feet. Dimitri scowls at me again, then flips me off. I return the gesture before making my way through the keep. I could portal my way to my bedroom, but the walk will do me good. At least, I'm hoping it will. The more time I spend alone in my bed, the harder it is to push Clara from my mind.

Even after a month in Hell, I'm still thinking about her. She hasn't summoned me and it's starting to grate on me. Some humans have reservations about sex. Witches are usually more open about bedroom activities.

I probably should have left when I noticed what she was doing. Her embarrassment has clearly derailed our short-lived relationship. Not that we were linked like that. I'm merely a demon she summoned to open a fucking jar for her. We're not connected beyond that. The thread tying us together must be linked to the summoning and nothing more.

Except that night with the desk. She didn't ask me to put it together. At the time, I hid behind the want to skip out on a meeting. It was more than that, though. Admitting it to Clara wasn't an option. I have no idea what she'd do with the information.

If I told her I was bored and I actually liked being there, she'd...probably do nothing. I convinced myself she'd mock me, but that's not like her. She might give me shit about it, just like Dimitri would. Taunting me wouldn't be her style. I couldn't bring myself to say anything. So, I cited paperwork and a meeting. And then I put together her desk without her asking. In fact, she told me I didn't have to. I'm loath to admit it, but that night was relaxing—fun.

And then I fucked it all up the next morning.

I don't blame her for not summoning me again. I could check on her—make sure she's okay. Except I shouldn't care. I *don't* care. I'm just pissed I don't have a place to hide out any longer. She was a small blip in my very long existence. She'll fade into the ether of my memories before long. Turns out, I'm really good at lying to myself.

There's a tug in my navel and I groan. Merely thinking about Clara wouldn't summon me. If that were the case, I'd be over there every half hour—maybe less. Yet here I am, being yanked through dimensions. I close my eyes, muttering under my breath all the things I can't tell her. I need to get it out of my system before I get to her house.

I grit my teeth as I drop into the summoning circle. Despite my weeks away, the chalk lines are fresh and my heart clenches. Maybe it's only been a few hours here. Fuck, I hate this shit. I rub my chest and hope the feeling goes away. My life is in enough upheaval without adding heart palpitations to the mix. Demons don't even get sick. If I walk back into Hell complaining of chest pains, Dimitri's going to have a field day.

A shiver rolls through me as I step out of the circle and prowl through the now-familiar house. A string of curses echoes through the living room, leading me toward her bedroom. At least she's not touching herself this time. I adjust myself as I walk down the hallway. I won't be able to hide how hard I am, but she seems preoccupied.

I knock softly, then push the door open an inch. "Clara?"

She moans, yet there's no pleasure in it this time around. "I didn't even say your name."

"Would you like me to go?" I grimace at my formal tone.

Why the fuck am I so nervous? I'm a fucking demon, not a novice. I've taken out entire armies—men and demons alike. My entire existence is predicated on being terrifying and confident. Yet here I am, asking her whether or not she wants me to go. She sounds sick, or hurt, and I can't bring myself to leave her like that unless she banishes me.

I wince when she moans again. "I'm coming in."

"Don't bother," she mutters, but I'm already shoving the door open.

She's curled in a ball on her side in the center of her bed. Moonlight streams through her window, illuminating her flushed face. A whimper escapes her and my feet move before I've convinced myself to interfere. My knee hits the mattress and her body rolls toward me slightly. Her arms tighten around her waist and she buries her face into the comforter.

"What's wrong?" I demand, brushing her dark hair away from her face. She's not sweating and she doesn't seem to have a fever.

"Nothing," she gasps.

"The fuck it is. You're clearly in pain." I slide my hand to her cheek and force her to look at me. "Was it Brandon? Did he fucking hurt you?"

She squints, then shakes her head. My shadows lash around me, coalescing into bands that reach for her. I attempt to rein them in, but I'm too close to the edge. They wrap around her, seeking to soothe her. It won't work. Not with the scenarios rolling through my mind. Whatever that fucker did, he'll pay. I should have dealt with him before. I didn't think he'd have the balls to come back, especially after I threatened him.

I lean down and my lips brush her temple. "I'll be back."

My nostrils flare as I straighten, not willing to admit why I did that. It wasn't a full on kiss, but it was enough. Clara's hand snaps out and her fingers grip my wrist. She's scowling at me again as if she'll be able to stop me through the power of her angst. The thought has me fighting a smirk.

"You will not go kill Brandon. It wasn't him. No one hurt me."

"Why are you protecting him? He's just a human piece of—"

Her face screws up and she groans, her nails digging into my skin. "Not protecting. It's that time of the month."

"What time? It's sunset right now."

"Fucking A," she breathes.

"Who's A? Is that who hurt—"

"No one's hurting me. Fuck me."

"Doubt you'd want me to fuck you while you're writhing in pain."

She rolls her eyes and lets go of me to flop onto her back. She grimaces and pulls her knees up. My hand twitches by my side and I resist the urge to strip her down. The sooner I find her wounds, the sooner I'll figure out what happened to her. I might not be able to heal her, but I could take out whoever hurt her. I'll make sure no one ever touches her again.

"Leave it to a demon to only have one thing on their mind." Her lids droop over her tired eyes. "I'm on my period, Omen. No one hurt me other than my own fucking body. Now go away so I can die a slow death in peace."

Shadowy tendrils weave through the air and settle over her

hands pressed against her stomach. I hate when they take on a life of their own, but I realize they're trying to soothe her in some way I can't understand. Mostly because I have no idea what her period is. If it's killing her, though, I need to fix it. Which means taking her to Hell or bringing someone here who can deal with whatever's ravaging her body.

"You're not allowed to die, little witch." I lean on the bed again, intent on picking her up when she bats my hands away.

"I'm not actually dying. I'm being dramatic. I'm on my period. I'll be fine by tomorrow. Maybe the next day." She scowls at me, then rolls off the bed. She doubles over and groans. I clamber around the mattress, desperation gripping me as she straightens and presses her knuckles to her temples.

"I'm taking you to Hell," I growl, reaching for her.

"Uh, the fuck you are," she snaps. "Seriously, have you never seen a woman on her period?"

I drop my hands to my sides and tilt my head. "This happens to others?"

She huffs. "Yes. Anyone with a uterus. Wait, do you know what a uterus is?"

I scowl, crossing my arms over my chest. "Yes, I know female anatomy."

"Well, then you should know...oh sweet goddess. Menses. Menstruating. The red wave. Aunt Flo. Period. They're all the same. Get it now?"

She stomps toward the bathroom and shuts the door behind her. It's not often I'm shocked. I thought I was immune to such things. At every turn, my little witch proves me wrong. It should be annoying.

If someone would have asked me weeks ago, I would have agreed how irritating it was to be summoned over and over again. Looking back, it's exhilarating in a way I haven't felt in a long time. Back when my existence was just beginning, I was enamored with finding the exciting parts—learning new things. Clara summoning me brought back that feeling I'd lost centuries ago.

I'm not ready to let the emotion go yet.

Convincing myself this is a bad idea doesn't work. I wrap my shadows around me and wink out of existence. I don't know if it's the nervous energy or the fact I just came from Hell, but the journey back is quick and painless. My head swims as the familiar obsidian walls rise around me. My feet slam into the rock, and Dimitri stumbles back.

"Tell me everything you know about mensurating. Now."

CHAPTER ELEVEN
CLARA

I hate having my period. Some of my friends have it worse and I always feel bad about complaining. It's probably why I tried to brush Omen off. Then again, he thought I was dying, so it seemed appropriate at the time. I'm regretting it now. Which is why I'm hiding in the bathroom. I don't even know why he's here. Unless I was mumbling his name in my sleep, he shouldn't be here.

My nose wrinkles as I pop some meds into my mouth. My cramps have been wreaking havoc on my body the entire day and my back aches. I want to shower, but the thought of going through the work of getting in, not to mention everything afterward, has me hesitating. It's too much, especially with Omen on the other side of the door.

Slowly, I turn the knob and peek into my bedroom. Omen doesn't rush me, and I inch the wood open more. Nothing. No shuffling, no curses, no Omen. He vanished as quickly as he appeared, apparently. I suppose I could take a shower now that he's gone. Still doesn't help with the actual act of showering, though. I squeeze my eyes shut, willing away the pain in my head.

I'm exhausted, my muscles ache, and all I want to do is sleep. I was trying to when Omen showed up. Not summoning him over the last month has taken its toll on me. I didn't think it would be so hard since we're not really friends. That argument doesn't hold weight anymore. I've spent more time with him than anyone else in a long time.

When he showed up and put together the desk, something changed. Or maybe it was when he saved me from the washing machine. I'm studiously ignoring the last time he was here. If I pretend he didn't catch me touching myself, then it didn't happen. Until I got my period, I refused to have any alone time. It's the fucking worst. Especially since I've been dreaming of Omen every damn night.

Another round of cramps batters me, and I sway as a wave of lightheadedness hits me. I collapse on my bed and curl into a ball again. It feels like my organs are strangling each other. Who knows which one will win out.

I should be pissed Omen walked out without so much as a *hope you feel better*. He merely enters a long line of squeamish men who are skeeved out by a little blood. He may be a demon, but he's as predictable as the humans around me.

My vision darkens, though I'm not sure how that's possible with only the moon lighting my room. Shadows softly cocoon me like a warm hug. A sigh leaves me and the sharp pain in my back eases. It's still there, but it doesn't feel like I'm being stabbed with a dull pencil anymore. Relief floods me as my muscles relax.

The mattress bounces and I grumble under my breath. Omen's cat has been randomly showing up. He yowls at me to feed him or to pet him or to open the window. I've also had to buy about seventeen different types of food. It's annoying, but then he looks at me with that little squished face and I cave.

"Go away, Pretty Boy," I groan.

"That my new nickname, little witch?" Omen whispers, his breath ghosting along the shell of my ear.

"What do you want?" I snap, then immediately regret my tone. It's not Omen's fault I'm in pain. It's not even his fault he left when he did.

"I got you some things." He brushes hair away from my face, and I peek at him. "Do you want to see now or later?"

"What's wrong with your face?" His horns wink in and out of existence. His silver hair flashes dark, then brown, then back to silver. If I didn't know any better, I'd think he was glitching out.

Omen shakes his head and he's engulfed in a dense mist. I can barely make out his silhouette, though I'm pretty sure his wings burst from his back, then disappear again. When the room clears, he's back to normal. At least, normal for him. His eyes flash red, dark pinpricks gazing back at me.

"Better?"

"What the fuck was that?"

He shrugs, then paws through the plastic bags spread at my feet. "I popped down to Hell, then topside, then back here. I had to shield the humans from my true form."

"Is that what you did with Brandon?"

He scowls, gritting his teeth. "Don't say that asshole's name." He grips my chin and his thumb brushes over my lower lip. "I don't ever want to hear his name fall from your lips again, do you hear me?"

I nod, then swallow hard. His eyes darken to full black, and I'm caught in his gaze. I couldn't look away even if I wanted to. Which I definitely do not. This is a fantasy straight from my dreams playing out. Maybe I *am* dreaming. I'm fast asleep, tucked under my covers while my brain protects me from the cramps ravaging my body. That would explain the desire dripping in his eyes. It would account for the parting of his mouth and the rapid pulse fluttering at his throat.

"I need your words, little witch," he breathes. "Do you understand what I expect from you?"

"Yes, sir."

"Good girl," he murmurs.

Thankfully, he pulls away to dig through the plastic bags so he doesn't see my full-body shudder. Who the fuck talks like that? I don't usually get worked up while on my period, but clearly my body didn't get the message. I could blame it on the fact he's a

demon, or maybe it's just him. Convincing myself not to lust after Omen hasn't worked one bit.

I sit up and my stomach cramps. I can't tell whether it's from hunger or my period. Doesn't matter since the thought of eating makes me nauseous. Or maybe that's the migraine forming in the back of my head. His little display distracted me from my cramps, but not for long.

"So, I have chocolate, alcohol, water, drugs, potatoes, and whatever these are." He holds up a box of tampons and I press my lips together.

I crawl to the edge of the bed and peek over the side. There's at least thirty boxes of tampons, pads, and menstrual cups scattered across my floor. Another bag has three bags of chips and three types of raw potatoes. I swear there's some frozen fries tucked underneath it all.

"Um, where did you get all this?"

"The food place. Dimitri called it a..." He grins, snapping his fingers and flames flicker up his arm. "Grocery store."

"Dimitri is your friend? Your demon friend I made fries for?"

He scowls, refusing to meet my eyes. "Yes, that's the one. He knew more about mensurating than I do."

I swallow a giggle. "Menstruating."

"Close enough. Now which—"

"It is not close enough. One is the shedding of the lining in the uterus and the other is something about measuring things, I'm pretty sure." I roll around until I'm sitting and grip a pillow in my lap. I don't know why, but it helps.

He huffs and his shadows gather near his ass, forming into a tail. I open my mouth to ask about it, but he shakes the box at me.

"I didn't know as much about periods. Better? Now, which do you need?" He gazes down at the many types of hygiene products.

"Did you buy the entire store? Seriously, no one within a twenty-mile radius will have—is that a pregnancy test?" I scramble off the bed and start digging through everything.

"I didn't buy all of it. Just one of each. And that thing"—he points at the pregnancy test—"was next to everything else. Dimitri said there were a lot of options and I shouldn't get the wrong one."

I press my lips together, keeping another giggle inside as I hold up a small box. "And this?"

He tilts his head and narrows his dark eyes. "I don't know what that is. It was on the top shelf. I only got one of them, though. The others looked...questionable."

"Oh? A vibrator looked questionable? Gotcha."

"What is it?"

I bite my lip and hide my face until I've straightened my face out. "This is for personal time. Tell me I don't have to explain that."

It hits me then that I should probably be embarrassed. Not because I'm holding a sex toy he bought, but because the last time I saw him, he caught me with a vibrator. Clearly he didn't see underneath the sheets. Maybe he's trolling me and I completely missed it.

"You don't have to explain personal time," he murmurs, smirking, and my cheeks flame.

I drop the box among the others and tuck my chin to my chest. I don't need him to see me wincing and think it's something other than more pain. He'll probably try to weasel a confession out of me or make some ridiculous comment again. He seems to like messing with me. It's the only explanation I can come up with for his borderline flirting.

Calling me a good girl wasn't him hitting on me. Normally, I wouldn't be so adamant, even to myself, about someone's intentions. I'd just ask them what their endgame was. Except Omen is a demon—one I forced to be here. They don't want to be with witches. We're a step above humans in their eyes, not quite as disdained, but enough to stay away from.

I swallow hard and press a fist against my stomach. "Thank

you for all this. You didn't have to do all this. And you don't have to wait around here. I'm sure—"

"Stop telling me I have better things to do," he growls. He gathers up all the items and arranges them on one side of the room.

"You don't have to do that."

His shoulders stiffen, his tail lashing back and forth, then he spins around. I don't have time to protest before he picks me up and sets me in the middle of the mattress. I get half a squawk out when he flips the covers over my body, leaving only my head exposed. He stomps back to his self-imposed job of sorting things.

"Tell me which ones you use," he demands.

I'm afraid to say anything so I just point at one of them. He snatches up the box and raises an eyebrow. I nod and he stomps off to the bathroom. I flip onto my side away from the door and pull my knees to my chest.

Another wave of dull pain washes over me, and I bury my face in the pillow. I thought the meds I took earlier would help, but my aches are back with a vengeance. I just have to wait for the wave to be over and my cramps will settle into the background. Hopefully, I'll be able to fall asleep and everything will be fine when I wake up.

"Sleeping won't make me go away, little witch."

"What exactly do you want me to do, Omen? You threatened to kill someone, bought me supplies, then put me to bed. The only time I've gotten any relief was when the damn cat showed up, but it was you. So, excuse me for not knowing what the fuck I'm supposed to do."

"None of that made any sense, but that's fine. You're clearly still in pain so I'll excuse your behavior."

I launch upright, a growl rumbling through the room. "I will gut you if you use that patronizing tone again, demon. Until you've felt what I currently do, you have no room to criticize my tone or words."

He holds up his hands and his throat bobs. "I didn't mean it like that."

"Then how exactly did you mean it?" My challenge hangs between us and his mouth flops open like a fish out of water. Of course he doesn't have an answer. Because he was being an asshole. He's not the first person I've encountered who's dismissed my pain and called me out on what they perceive to be a shitty attitude. And he won't be the last.

He steps closer and I tense. When he settles on the bed next to me, I lean away from him. I still don't understand why he's here—why he stuck around. He didn't have to check on me. He didn't have to go to the store for me. He didn't have to do any of this. All I've done to repay him is snap at him and give him a halfhearted thanks.

Tears well up in my eyes, and I glance away. I fucking hate feeling like I don't know my own emotions. I want to be pissed at him. I want to be left alone. I want to be held and told everything will be fine. I want to be fed a pint of ice cream. I don't know what I want.

"Hey," he whispers. His hand slides along my cheek and turns me towards him. "I shouldn't have said that. I apologize. I meant I don't blame you for being in a shitty mood. The last time I was hurt, I was in the worst mood and had no one there to bitch at. I wish someone would have taken my bullshit."

I sniff. "Where was Dimitri?"

He lets out a humorless laugh. "He was worse off than I was. I couldn't complain to him."

"I didn't think demons got hurt. Aren't you, like, indestructible?"

His hand drops from my face and disappointment lances through me. "I think you're mistaking indestructible with immortal. Neither of which we are, actually. But that's a conversation for another time. What do you need right now?"

I search my mind, trying to find one thing I can ask him for that won't be too much of a burden. I should tell him I'm fine and there's nothing he can do. Except I'm so tired of doing everything alone. My family is gone and my friends are off living their own lives. I want a companion.

I doubt Omen would choose me, even if sex wasn't on the table, but he's here now and he hasn't run yet. In fact, he ran *to* me. He could have skipped out and he didn't. For now, he chose me and that's enough.

"Will you just stay until I fall asleep?" Having him here might be enough. "But wake me up when you go. Just enough so I'm not freaked out if I wake up later and find out you're gone."

His brows pull low and I brace myself for him to deny me. If he walks away, I'll let him go without a fight. I'll take the rejection like I do everyone else's, with poise and silence. I'll vow to never summon him again, no matter how many sauce jars I need opened. It takes everything in me not to tell him it's fine and he can go. Instead, I wait patiently for him to poof out of existence.

He pats the pillow behind me, and I sink onto my back. My lip ends up between my teeth, and he scowls until I stop. After he's tucked me in, he pushes to his feet and my eyes slam closed. No use watching him leave and maybe I'll be able to hide the shame flooding my system.

"Move over," he grunts, and my lids fly open.

I scoot toward the side of the bed and he slides in next to me. He radiates heat, and I desperately want to press my body to his. Except I'm not weird like that. Other ways, sure, but not that. I flip to my side, my back facing him. My efforts are for naught. His arm slips around my waist and he tugs me close to him. Instantly, my lids droop and my muscles relax. Even my cramps ease into the background and my headache vanishes.

A sigh leaves me and I slide into dreamland, telling myself I'll ask him if he's a healer later.

CHAPTER TWELVE
OMEN

Clara's breath evens out and I let out a sigh. I can't relax, though. I'm desperately trying to keep my hips away from her ass. She definitely doesn't need to wake up with my hard cock poking her back. It's not like I can just will my erection away, especially with her body pressed against mine. She has no idea what she's doing to me. I don't blame her.

From what Dimitri told me, periods aren't fun. He went off on a tangent about different levels of pain and how some don't get it that bad. I tuned him out, then popped topside when he was mid-sentence.

A shudder runs through me when I remember my time at the store. The lights were too bright, the choices too many, and the workers gave me a wide berth. I wasn't surprised. Even with a mask over my features, humans have enough sense to steer clear of a demon. Which meant I wandered around forever trying to find everything. I stood in front of the boxes of tampons for much too long. I overheard one woman say some of them were pads. That was about the time I started filling the cart with one of everything. Some of them didn't make sense to me—the cups, the vibrator, the test. They were all next to each other on the shelves, though, so I just got it all. Minus the ones that looked like fake cocks. I never thought I'd be jealous of a piece of what looked like rubber, but here we are.

Clara mumbles in her sleep, and I tighten my grip on her. I shush her, my lips brushing her temple. She settles and my chest aches, though I don't know why. Or maybe I'm just not ready to admit it.

I close my eyes, attempting to sleep. Every time Clara shifts, my eyes snap open. She turns in my arms and tucks her head under my chin. My hand rests on her lower back and she moans. I swallow hard and bury my nose in her hair. I should leave or at least retreat to the chair in the corner of her room. Instead of listening to my better judgment, I pull her closer.

Hours pass, marked only by the moon marching across the dark hardwood floors. My lids droop and I float between waking and sleeping. Every shift of her body snaps me awake.

"This is all Dimitri's fault," I say under my breath.

The air around me thickens and my nostrils flare. My gaze skips around the room, waiting for something to jump out of the dark corners. My shadows envelop Clara, hiding her from the threat stalking us.

My growl rumbles through the room as Dimitri's grinning face steps out of the blackness. He isn't fazed by my obvious displeasure, merely waving away my shadows so he can get a clear view of Clara. He's powerful enough to walk through my magic. I always thought it was helpful, but now I'm having second thoughts.

"What the fuck are you doing here?" I snarl.

"No idea. Haven't been summoned in a hot minute, but suddenly here I was. Thought your witch wanted a sexier demon to look at." He grins as I glare daggers at him. "Oh, don't be like that. Such a grump. Ope, and possessive."

"I'm not possessive," I whisper harshly. "And keep your voice down."

Gently, I ease away from Clara, and she reaches for me. I smooth her hair away from her forehead, and she tugs a pillow into her to replace me.

Dimitri sidles up next to me. "Jealous of a pillow? Don't blame you. She's cu—"

I snatch his arm and march him out of her bedroom, down the hallway, and into the living room. I snap my fingers and a lamp in the corner flares to life. The desk I put together sits under the window looking out on the front lawn. She hasn't moved too much around, but enough to change the entire feel of the place. For some reason it pisses me off.

"You've spent a lot of time here, huh?" Dimitri murmurs as he pokes around the room.

"Get out of her things," I growl. "What are you doing here?"

"She sells plants? Using her witchy skills. Smart." He spins around and smirks. "I already told you. Got the ole summons and here I am."

"Well, no one summoned you. Clara is sleeping and has been for a while, and I certainly can't do that shit. So, go back."

He winces and I brace myself. "Uh, I tried that. Didn't work. Not entirely sure *who* summoned me, but I can't go back. Might work if your witch girlfriend did it. You want me to wake her up or..."

"She's not my girlfriend. You're not waking her up. It's five in the morning here and she didn't get to sleep until late. Just...crash here or something."

"So you can go back to cuddling?" His gaze drops, reminding me I'm in only underwear, and he smirks. "Kind of cute how she was all tucked into you. Been a while since I've been with a witch. How is it?"

I scrub my hands down my face and groan. "I haven't bedded her. And I don't plan on it. She's not my girlfriend and I wasn't cuddling. What the fuck is wrong with you?"

"Me?" He plasters on an innocent face like I can't see right through him. "What's wrong with *you*? She's been summoning you for weeks now, which most people would consider flirting, yet here you are missing all the many signs she's throwing out. Also, no one calls it bedding anymore. You really need to spend more time topside if this is going to work out."

"I'm not doing this with you. Crash on the couch or go wander around until she's awake."

"Why are you so against this?"

I stomp past him, but his hand snaps out and grabs me. "Let go."

"Omen, we've known each other for centuries. Tell me what the fuck is wrong with you."

I peel his fingers from my arm and round on him. "Did you ever think that not all of us are so cavalier with our relationships? Maybe we don't all just want to fuck, then fuck off."

"Hey," he says weakly.

I know I'm hurting him, but I can't stop. Everything I've kept inside, everything I've been avoiding, bubbles within me. He started this, forcing me to share shit I never wanted to even think about. He may not deserve it, but he opened this can of worms.

"And let's say I throw caution to the wind. What then? She's topside. She has a life here. She has fucking friends." I jab my fingers at the photo hanging on her wall. "I'm a damn demon who lives in Hell. What exactly do you expect me to do? Kidnap her? Bring her down to Hell and force her to be there with me? Just hoping she'd eventually want to stay. Oh, and I'd either have to convince her to give up her mortality or watch her grow old at an expedited rate until she wastes away to nothing. Do I have that right or am I missing something?"

Shock splashed across Dimitri's face makes me pause. "You really went down the rabbit hole, didn't you? Fuck, Omen. I was just teasing. Not like I expected you to be soulbound to her."

"Ludo would have my ass if I was," I mutter.

I didn't even think about mating her. Binding her to me forever seems extreme, especially since we haven't even fucked yet.

"Well, whatever you do, you might want to figure it out quick. Your absence has been noted."

"I'm not—"

Dimitri vanishes in a puff of purple smoke, taking the light from the lamp with him. I tip my head back and sigh heavily. Ever since Clara summoned me, I've been off-kilter. My sleep schedule is the least of my concerns, but I'm convinced if I just crashed for a day or two, my mind wouldn't be as muddled. I could figure out everything else at that point.

"Omen?" Clara calls softly, and I turn. "I thought you were going to wake me when you left? Why does it smell like sulfur?"

Her messy dark hair creates a halo around her head. The moon has long since set, hiding from the sun's eventual coming. Despite the shadows, I swear her silhouette glows with an inner light I didn't notice before. I don't think she notices either. She rubs her hands up and down her arms, then grips her elbows. Her gaze skips around the room, never settling on me for long, and I realize I haven't answered her.

"I didn't leave. I thought I heard the cat." I stroll close to her. "Turns out it was nothing. Let's go back to bed."

She lets me lead her back to the bedroom. She doesn't question me about the sulfur again. I don't know why, but I'd rather not mention Dimitri's visit. Regardless of why he was here, it has nothing to do with Clara. She slides between the sheets and blinks lazily at me. A question rests in her eyes and relief floods them when I slip in next to her. I'm playing a dangerous game with my restraint.

She doesn't hesitate to cuddle close to me and my arms wrap around her. Her heart thunders against my chest, giving her away. Soon, it slows and her muscles relax. When I think she's asleep, I roll onto my back, keeping my arm behind her back. I jolt when she huffs.

"Why are you lying to me?" she whispers.

"What do you think I lied about?"

"The sulfur. It's the same smell when you poof. You avoided the question."

My fingers brush along her side and she shivers. "Dimitri was here. Then he left. I didn't want you to think random demons would be showing up."

"Except he's your friend, so he's not really random. What did he need? Shit, you need to go back, don't you?"

She attempts to push away from me, making me cling tighter to her. Everything I spouted off to Dimitri was the truth. Except I can't seem to let her go. All my plans to sever the tie between us flew out the window. I haven't even thought about it since I put together her desk. No matter how much being with her wouldn't work in the long term, I'm hesitant to let her go completely.

"I don't need to be anywhere. He doesn't know why he got sent here, and he got sent...somewhere else."

"Shit, do I need to get rid of the summoning circle?" She pushes again as if she'll get up right now and wash away the evidence.

"If you erase the circle, you won't be able to summon *any* demons." I hold my breath, hoping she understands the implications. I won't stop her if she wants to go through with it. I can't.

My arm falls away from her as she scrambles to her feet. She grabs a silk robe and slides her arms into the sleeves. I prop myself against the headboard, the sheet settling around my hips. I refuse to chase after her. If she wants to erase me from her life, then so be it.

I'm too far gone to think it won't hurt, but eventually I'll get over it. At least I hope I will. Maybe she'll plague the rest of my existence. She'll sit in the back of my mind, a reminder of all the ways I went wrong. She'll torment my waking hours and haunt my dreams every night. It'll be an apt punishment for thinking a witch like her would ever want a demon like me.

She's almost out the door when she stops and glances over her shoulder. "Aren't you coming?"

"Not anytime soon, little witch." My attempt at a joke falls flat. I clear my throat and mutter, "I'll wallow here instead."

"What if I need help?"

"You won't need my help. Actually, I can't." I doubt the

magic would allow me to participate in erasing my existence from this plane. I don't know the consequences, especially since she used that damned book. The thing has a vindictive side.

She turns, confusion splashed across her face. "What do you mean, you can't?"

"No demons, Clara. None."

She tilts her head, and I see the exact moment it clicks. She nods once, then spins around and stomps out of the room. My eyes slam shut and I wait for the familiar tug to drag me back to Hell.

CHAPTER THIRTEEN
CLARA

"I shouldn't be doing this," I whisper as I dig around in the canning cellar.

It's not technically a cellar. This house doesn't have a large basement, only three small rooms tucked behind thick wooden doors. I doubt I'll find what I'm looking for in here. Most of the shelves are empty now, marking the end of my mother's influence over my food choices. Pain stabs at my heart at the thought, yet I shove the grief deep down.

I huff, then shove the door shut and move on to the next closet. Old paint cans and random tile samples fill the room. I don't know what exactly I'm looking for, but I keep grabbing various containers. One after another, they all fail me. I push aside a paint roller and it clatters to the concrete floor.

A chill snakes up my spine, leading to a full-body shudder. I should have put on slippers and maybe a sweatshirt. Anything would be better than this thin robe. I miss Omen's radiating heat. I wonder if controlling fire is something all demons can do or if it's just Omen. There's so much about him I don't know, yet it's like he's been part of my life forever.

"Ridiculous," I mutter.

"What's ridiculous?" A deep voice asks from behind me and I spin around, a scream escaping me.

Demon. Not Omen, obviously. His dark skin lacks a reddish

tint and he doesn't have tattoos. No horns. No wings. No shadows. He grins, revealing a sharp row of teeth. I wince and they disappear. Not behind his lips, but into regular teeth one would find in a human. He must be masking his true form, but why?

I hold my hands up as if that will stop him from attacking me. I swallow hard and the cans rattle as my back hits the shelves. Alarm flashes in his eyes. Or maybe hunger. I'm not exactly in the right mind to gauge someone's feelings.

Omen. My mouth forms his name, yet no sound comes out. Maybe I can summon him through sheer willpower or speaking to him through my mind.

"Oh, that's a witch's scared face. My bad." He backs away, and I suck in a sharp gasp. I didn't even realize I was holding my breath. "I'm Dimitri. Did Omen tell you about me? Or does that mean absolutely nothing to you? Shit."

"You're Dimitri?" I croak.

"Yup, that's me." He grins again as I drop my hands onto my knees and attempt to calm my racing heart. "You good? Where's Omen? Should I get him?"

"You ask too many questions," I wheeze.

He steps closer and I tense, forcing him to retreat once more. "Can't get answers without asking the right questions. What are you looking for?"

"Lacquer. Or maybe some clear glue."

"You going to erect"—he snorts and I roll my eyes—"a statue in Omen's honor?"

"How the hell would I make a statue out of lacquer? No, I'm going to pour it over the summoning circle so I don't lose it."

His eyebrows disappear beneath a flop of dark hair. "Well, that is certainly interesting."

"Can you, like, pop out to the store and get me something?"

Should I be asking a random demon I just met to do me a favor? No. Probably not. My chest tightens and I straighten. I've only asked Omen for favors, though he made it seem like he had to. Other than the desk, I basically forced him to do chores for me. He might still hate it and doesn't want me to preserve the summoning circle.

Dimitri opens his mouth, and I shake my head. "Actually, no. I'm fine. Why are you here? Omen said you left."

"Oh no, no. You don't get to change the subject like that."

"I most certainly do. This is my house and you came through my summoning circle."

He holds up a finger. "Nope. I popped right into your bedroom." His eyes widen. "Not like that. I didn't...it wasn't on purpose. I don't know who summoned me, but you were sleeping. Then I just disappeared and was in a closet for however long. Now I'm back for whatever reason. I also can't leave without permission, I'm pretty sure."

"Okay, well, I give you permission to get the hell out of my house."

He smirks. "I can see why you get under Omen's skin."

My mouth drops open. "What the fuck is that supposed to mean?"

"Just that you're feisty. Probably keep him on his toes. Don't worry, sweetheart. I'm not complaining. He needs someone who will push back when he needs it—call him out on his bullshit. I try, but I'm not you." He crosses his arms, leaning against the door frame.

"I...that's not what's...I'm sorry. I don't know what Omen told you, but we're not...I just summoned him. Then basically trapped him here to do my chores." Whatever fight I had in me vanishes and my shoulders sag. "And I'm not your sweetheart."

"Duly noted," he murmurs.

I step away from the shelf. The room is so small I could reach out my hand and touch him. I won't, because that'd be weird, but still. The pull I've felt toward Omen isn't there with Dimitri. He doesn't give me creepy vibes. Not like Brandon. Yet it's nothing like what I feel for Omen.

"Is there something you need, because I don't think giving me advice will do anything," I snap, frustration lining my voice.

"Whoa there. A little advice never hurt anyone." He smiles, though it's nothing like the grin before. He reaches out, then pulls back when his hand brushes my arm. "I really think you should—"

"Dimitri," Omen growls from behind his friend. I can't see Omen's face, but he doesn't sound happy. Dimitri winces and the skin on his shoulders cracks open. I shake my head and squeeze my eyes shut. When I open them again, the illusion is gone, thankfully. I don't know how much more I can handle today.

Omen yanks Dimitri away and shoves him deeper into the basement against the third closet. There isn't much room for him to stuff himself into, and I almost feel bad for him. Then I catch sight of Omen's face and change my mind about saying something. Not only are his wings brushing the ceiling and his shadows curling around his body, but his tail lashes against the wall. He's glaring at me as if I did something.

"Upstairs. Now," he growls, his deep voice rumbling through me.

"Omen." Dimitri's tone holds a warning and Omen snarls, his eyes never leaving mine.

I cross my arms and glare at him. "No."

"I'm not in the mood for your attitude, little witch. Get upstairs before I throw you over my shoulder."

"Maybe *I'm* not in the mood for *your* attitude, *little demon*," I snap and Dimitri snorts. It's not the best comeback, but it's the only one I got. "Besides, you wouldn't dare treat me like a sack of potatoes."

The corner of his mouth twitches. "Wouldn't dare?"

"I am a witch, if you'll remember. I doubt you'd appreciate ephelides all over your body."

His eyes narrow and Dimitri lets out a wheezing cough. Omen doesn't even spare him a glance, though he should. His friend sounds like he's going to keel over any minute.

I lean forward, trying to get Dimitri in my eyeline. Omen slides

forward and fills the doorway to block my view. I don't know why he's acting like a jealous asshole. Or maybe it has nothing to do with jealousy and everything to do with the overlap of his two worlds colliding.

"Oh shit," Dimitri breathes, then poofs out of existence, leaving the tang of sulfur behind.

"Well, that solves that," I mutter.

I want to ask him why he's acting like he caught his friend and me making out. I won't because I'm a fucking coward. If I'm being honest, I'm afraid of his answer. He didn't even want to say Dimitri's name before, much less have me know they're friends. My mind runs over my conversation with the other demon. Random words stick out: feisty, Omen's skin, push back. None of it matters anyway.

"Go, Clara," Omen says, stepping aside. Weariness lines his voice and he pinches the bridge of his nose.

I open my mouth to snap at him or maybe to apologize. Slowly, I press my lips together and slink past him. Tonight hasn't gone the way I thought it would. Actually, I imagined wallowing in my pain, then forcing myself to get up tomorrow and shower. It's hard to think when your insides feel like they've grown spikes and are shredding your organs.

I turn at the bottom of the stairs and find him in the same position. "Thank you for bringing me all that stuff. And I'm sorry about Dimitri."

He doesn't move, doesn't even look at me. I swallow down all the things I want to say and all the questions I want to ask. If he's not going to say anything, then so be it.

I turn and walk up the stairs. He doesn't follow, because of course he doesn't. I wander back to my bedroom, wondering if I could actually fall asleep again. My gaze catches on the crumpled sheets and I sigh.

My knees crack as I drop in front of the plastic bags. I don't know how much time passes while I separate everything, but eventually I get to the ice cream. Tears fill my eyes as I take in the

massacre. When I lift the sack, a sticky mess spreads across the hardwoods.

"What the fuck," I breathe.

I can't be mad at Omen for not knowing ice cream melts if it's left out. The demon didn't know what fries were. Except now I don't have any and the last thing I want to do is go into town to get more. My cramps may be gone, but I just feel gross now. I'll clean myself up after I deal with this. I drop the bag, then push to my feet.

Every time I swipe my hand across my cheeks, they come away wet. I shouldn't be crying, but I can't seem to stop. If I keep moving, eventually it'll end and I'll forget why I'm blubbering. I end up using an entire roll of paper towels in my quest to clean everything. I'm still scrubbing the dark floor when a meow echoes from behind me.

A heavy sigh leaves me. "Hey, Handsome. I'll feed you in a little bit. Just give me a minute."

A teardrop hits the floor and I wipe it away. Another one drips off my nose and I wipe that one away, too. The more I try to push Omen from my mind, the more he fills it. I thought things between us were changing last night. I didn't think I was an obligation to fulfill. Looking back, that's exactly what I am to him. I shouldn't be surprised he told me to get rid of the summoning circle.

Handsome butts his head against my hip, and I drop the sopping wet towel. It's not doing any good anyway. I gather the cat in my arms and bury my face in his fluffiness. My muscles relax while my chin quivers. His purrs reverberate through my chest. A choked sob leaves me. Not for Omen. Not only for Omen. Despair fills me at the direction my life has taken. I thought I was content before Omen showed up, and I blamed him for my turmoil. It's not his fault, though. It's mine.

I forgot what it's like to be alone. Once I moved away from my hometown, I didn't know anyone. Sure, I could still call home, but eventually that stopped. Dad passed, then Mom. Friends got

me through since I didn't have anyone else. Then I lost my job and ended up isolated in my house, trying to figure out what I wanted out of life. My friends started dropping off, one by one. I keep coming back to them moving on when I feel like I'm stuck. Then I feel guilty for thinking they should put their lives on hold merely to include me.

"It'll be okay, Kitty Cat," I wheeze. "Everything will be—"

The cat disappears in a puff of smoke, leaving my arms empty. Shock spreads through me and dries up my tears. I'm not even surprised. Of course the cat would leave when Omen does. It's his fucking pet. Except now I have a shit ton of cat food, toys, and a bed without anything to show for it. I'll have to donate everything to the shelter, which means I'll have to drive an hour to the nearest one. I swear I spent hundreds of dollars on random things and now I have to purge my house.

I swallow hard and concentrate on my breathing. Anything to keep me from spiraling. I need to get my shit together and figure out my future. Wallowing isn't my style and I don't know why I've been stuck in this hole for so long. I could blame my hormones, or my friends, or Omen, but really it's me and I'm tired. I'm exhausted with myself, honestly. Being a whiny bitch isn't fun.

Whatever happens, I'll be fine. My days will settle into a routine and everything will go back to normal—a different normal, but that's fine. My family is gone. My friends are gone. My cat is gone. Omen is...he's gone.

And I'll be perfectly fine.

CHAPTER FOURTEEN
OMEN

My feet slam into the obsidian floor in the main hall of Hell. Shards fling into the wall, the chairs, the others gathered around. Demons scatter as I stalk across the large room and smoke rolls through the sky of the open ceiling. Fire drips from my fingertips and I relish the heat searing through my body.

Normally, I'd quash the need to explode, knowing how dangerous it is for those around me, not to mention myself. This time, I fan the flames, letting them consume whatever logical ideas my mind throws at me.

The crowd parts, leaving only Dimitri in my path. When he turns, he only has time to widen his eyes before my hand latches onto his throat and I slam him into the pillar behind him. He struggles for a minute, then sags in my grasp. He knows he won't be able to get away from me. Not without hurting himself. He'd have to call down lightning to even come close, and he won't do that. He understands this.

"Get on with it," he wheezes and his skin cracks, revealing deep purple underneath. Sparks crackle along the grooves, and I snarl at him.

"You touched her," I snarl.

"Barely."

I lean closer as I attempt not to suffocate him with my flames. I may be pissed at him, but I don't want to kill him. He's still my oldest friend. One of my *only* friends. Which is why I'm so pissed at him.

I told him about Clara in confidence. I didn't think he'd use the information against me. The betrayal cuts deep. My throat aches as fire creeps upward. My stomach rolls, a tug like the one I've felt so often recently hitting me hard. If she summons me right now, she won't like who she meets.

"Omen," he gasps, and I growl, launching us into the void.

Dimitri's high-pitched screams echo around us, then cut off abruptly when we land in his rooms. I throw him onto his bed and he screams again.

"Knock it off," I snap as I pace around the room. I shake out my hands, leaving burn marks in my wake.

"You're flaming out, Omen." Dimitri's voice holds a warning I'm desperately trying to heed.

He flings himself off the bed and crashes to the floor. His boots slip as he tries to scramble to his feet, and he hisses when a stray ember hits his shoulder. My vision dims as another wave of nausea hits me. I brace my hands on my knees and breathe through my nose. It doesn't help.

Movement from the corner of my eye has me turning my head, and I'm hit with a face full of water. Steam and sizzling fills the air, obscuring Dimitri. It doesn't help the burn in my veins, but at least I'm not in danger of burning down his quarters.

"I didn't touch her. Just a brush on her arm," he whispers. "You shouldn't be..."

As the air clears, I can finally see the indecision in his eyes. "Spit it out."

"You shouldn't be ready to kill me over that. You shouldn't be like...well, like *this* at all. You know what this is, Omen."

I shake my head, unable to give voice to my fears. Whatever he's about to say doesn't matter. It *can't* matter, because if it does, then my entire existence crumbles. Everything I've worked for will disappear, vanishing without a trace. I'll lose...her. She'll vanish and I'll end up in the void until I float away with no one to remember me. I'll fade from Dimitri's mind and be erased from every memory I've been in.

"Don't go near her," I snarl and prowl toward the door.

Dimitri steps in front of me, blocking my way. He always was better at traveling through the void between dimensions. My hands curl into fists and I glare at him as if I can get him to move through sheer force of will. If he doesn't move, I'm liable to burst into flames again, and I don't know if I'll be able to stop myself from taking him out.

"Move."

"No can do," he says, shaking his head. "You need to deal with this now or—"

"Or nothing. Move or I'll move you."

He rolls his eyes, and my shadows whip around me. "You can't use the same threats against me as you do your—"

My hand seizes his throat once more and he gags. "I'd advise you not to finish that sentence."

He grabs my wrist, but doesn't try to remove me. His gaze meets mine, pity and understanding mingling together. The truth sits there, mocking me, challenging me, warning me. I'm not ready. I'll never be ready.

I wrap my shadows around my body and vanish into the space between worlds. He can't follow me there. A swooping sensation hits me along with the ever-present tug of the thread between Clara and me. She isn't summoning me. I should be grateful for that, but a wave of sadness hits me out of nowhere. I doubt she'll call for me again unless it's a mistake.

Still, I follow the strand through the nothingness, unable to help myself. I don't have to show myself. I can merely hide behind a mask of invisibility, make sure she's okay, then come home. It'll put my nerves at ease, and I'll be able to let her go.

Except as soon as her house appears, I realize how fucked I am. I don't know how much time has passed, but it's no longer five in the morning. Bright sunlight streams through the trees, highlighting Clara's dark hair. She lets out a frustrated cry as she bats at the vines crawling up the side of her home. She jumps and latches onto a particularly stubborn one and yanks hard. It doesn't move, and she lets out a string of curses that would make most demons blush. An unbidden smile creeps up my face, and I fight against it.

My gaze travels over her form, and I forget every single reason why I shouldn't be here. Every argument I had against being with her vanishes, and I stalk forward. My muscles relax the closer I get, giving me a false sense of calm. I don't trust my own emotions when it comes to Clara.

"Bullshit vines," Clara mumbles under her breath. "Think you can come in here and just spread your tendrils around? Dig your way into my foundation? Damage my stucco? I don't fucking think so. You may have won the battle, but I'm definitely going to win the war. As soon as I get a ladder."

I snap my fingers and the vines disappear. Clara jumps and stumbles around, a shriek on her lips. Her very plump red lips.

"Omen? What are—Where did you..." She clamps her mouth shut and swallows hard, avoiding my eyes. "Thank you. You didn't have to do that."

Her tongue darts out and drags across her bottom lip, drawing my gaze down. I step closer and her spine snaps straight. Another one and she sways as if her body and mind are at war. Her hesitancy gives me pause. For some reason, I assumed she'd be riding the edge of sanity with me.

"Well, I didn't want to have to save you from falling off a ladder," I murmur with a smirk.

Her face hardens, and I realize I fucked up a second before her palms slam into my chest. "Fuck you, Omen. You think you can just pop in here after all this time with a snap of your fingers and a quippy joke? I don't think so."

She hits me again, and once more for good measure. Heat sears through me where her skin touches mine, and I realize I'm still in the sweatpants I summoned when I landed in Hell. I open my mouth to say something, *anything*, yet no words come out.

Her eyes narrow and she snatches gloves from her back pocket. She smacks me with them. I fight a smile and hold my hands up in surrender.

"Easy there, little witch. You'll take out an eye—"

She shrieks, throwing her hands up and pivoting away. A second later, she marches back to me and lets out a frustrated growl. I swear she's about to shake her fist at me. She stomps away again. I saunter toward the now-vineless wall and lean against it, resigning myself to waiting her out. Eventually, she'll run out of steam and we can actually talk.

"Ooh, you. Just when I was fine. Just when I didn't wake up in the middle of the night. Just when I stopped hearing that damn feline." She huffs, then kicks a stick at me. At least, I think she's trying to. The small branch doesn't even make it six inches. "No note. No cosmic sign. Just a whole helluva lot of silence." She jabs her finger at me. "Who in the hell gave you the right?"

I sober when I spot the sheen in her eyes. A single tear tips from her lid and trickles down her cheek. My fingers tingle and I resist the urge to grab her. Whether to shake the answers out of her or comfort her, I don't know.

"How long?" I rasp out.

"What?" she snaps as another tear falls.

"How long was I gone?"

Her lips purse and she pulls in a deep breath as if bracing herself for my naivety. "Six months."

"All this for a week?" I growl, prowling toward her.

"A week? No, asshole. Six. Months. As in twenty-six weeks. As in, one hundred and eighty-two days."

"Months."

My vision blurs and my stomach flips. I don't know how long I was between dimensions. Or how long it took me to get back to myself when I transported Dimitri and myself to his room. Magic gets wonky in Hell, twisting and warping at a whim. It has something to do with the balance, but I never bothered to find out. I wasn't assigned to the magical department for a reason.

"What happened?" she asks flatly.

I squeeze my eyes shut and flex my hands over and over in an attempt to center myself. "I followed Dimitri back to Hell. We had...words. Then I came back here."

"How long was it there?"

I shrug, not knowing how to explain time in a space that has none. I shouldn't have come here. Six months for humans is a long time. For demons, it's nothing. Even for a witch, six months is long enough for her to forget. She's moved on with her life and then I blast back in without a care in the world. All the reasons I was going to cut things off come rushing back to me.

I clear my throat as I stare at nothing. "I'm sorry."

There's nothing really more to say. I could give her excuses or convince her of...what? That we're connected in some magical way? No, she deserves more than whatever half-life I can offer. She'd be waiting around more than six months while I lost track of time in Hell. There's no path forward that allows her to be her own person. Besides, I don't need a witch in my life. The thought rings hollow and a hole opens in my chest.

I step to the side, intending to walk to the edge of her property before vanishing. She doesn't stop me. She's not even looking at me. I wonder if she even notices or if she's simply ignoring me. I don't blame her. I slide around her and make my way to the road.

Glancing over my shoulder, I clear my throat. "Might want to clean up the circle."

She lets out a frustrated groan, and I face forward. Should have kept my damn mouth shut. I wrap my shadows around me, trying to find comfort in them, when she shoves me from the back. I stumble, almost sprawling onto the dirt. She didn't hit me that hard, but I didn't expect her to smack me again.

"You don't get to walk away. You don't get to decide how this goes. I want to know why you left in the first place. I want to know why you freaked out when Dimitri showed up. I want to know why you stayed that night, then fucked off the next morning. You owe me that much."

I spin slowly. "Owe you?" I stalk closer and her spine snaps straight. "Careful, little witch."

"Or what?" she snarls, though there's a hesitancy to her words.

"I think you forget *you* summoned *me*. You drew the chalk and wrote my sigil. You asked for my help. And even when you didn't, I still saved you."

She sputters, desperately trying to keep hold of her anger. "Saved me? Opening a jar of spaghetti sauce can hardly be constituted as *saving* someone. And sure, the washer might have been trying to eat me, but I would have figured it out. I always do."

"Like you did with the desk? Or the vines? Or when you were dying?" For every step forward, she takes an equal one back until she ends up against the wall.

She huffs, avoiding my eyes. "I wasn't dying. I was on my period. And I was perfectly fine the next day."

"And why do you think that is?"

"Well, it certainly wasn't the melted ice cream I had to clean up from my floor. Or the dishes I had to do after making you fries. Or the—"

I hold up my hand, then rest my palms on either side of her head, boxing her in. "Are you done?"

Her chin tips up and she stares at me. "And if I'm not?"

I smirk and her throat bobs. I don't know what I'm doing, but I can't walk away from her now. Magic keeps my feet planted. Doesn't matter either way. There's nowhere else I'd rather be than right here bickering with her.

CHAPTER FIFTEEN
CLARA

This is it. The moment he walks away again. Or vanishes without an explanation. Or his cat will show up. Or Dimitri.

Something always gets in the way of whatever we're hurtling toward. The past six months were hell, no pun intended. I went through all the stages and came out the other side...not the best version of myself, but better. I was handling things. Then he shows up again and all the walls I built around myself crumbled. He didn't even have to do anything other than appear.

As much as I wanted to see him, I never said his name. I knew the moment I did, I'd be pissed at myself. Once someone leaves, I let them stay gone. Dragging them back into my life doesn't do anything other than hurt both of us. Omen doesn't want to be here.

Except he has that look in his eyes. The same one when he hauled my ass out from behind the washer and when he crawled into bed with me that last night. I always explained it away. I don't think I can anymore. And I don't want to. Being alone isn't fun and I don't want to do it anymore. So, I'll just let him do whatever he wants. If he walks away, I'll just pick up the pieces of my shattered heart once more.

My chest seizes at the thought. Did he break my heart? Have I fallen for him? We've barely spent any time together, which isn't

entirely accurate, I suppose. They feel like stolen moments and I'm the thief who took them. I hoarded them, convincing myself it was all I'd have to sustain me through the years. If he leaves again, I doubt he'll remember me. These times will fade for him, and I'll be nothing but a wisp of remembrance from a lifetime ago. He has an endless existence to forget people—including me.

"Going to tell me what's going on in that pretty little head of yours?" he murmurs, a smirk playing on his lips.

"Well, that was condescending," I mutter as I glance away. He hums and his fingers brush my hair behind my ear. I beat back a shudder, not willing to give in just yet. Not completely, though my resolve is crumbling pretty damn quickly.

"Yet my calling you little witch isn't? Explain that one."

I press my lips together. There isn't any difference, but I'm not about to admit it. He thinks he's so damn—his fingers grip my chin and he forces me to look at him. A smile slowly splits his lips and my heartbeat tap-dances out a lively rhythm in my chest. I swear I can hear music flitting through the air. It's lilting and lulls me into an unexpected semblance of tranquility. I don't know whether to trust it, but I don't think I care very much. As long as he keeps looking at me like he is and the melody continues and my heartbeat remains. As long as I can stay in this bubble of tranquility.

"You're awfully quiet. Time to make a decision, Clara."

"A decision about what?"

"Whether you're going to get rid of the summoning circle or keep it as is."

I huff out a breathless laugh. "Six months, Omen. I didn't get rid of it for six months and you're asking me if I'm going to do it now? Right after you showed up again?"

He shrugs and releases my chin before boxing me in again. "Why didn't you wash it away?"

"I couldn't," I whisper. "At first, I thought you'd come back. Then I was mad at you even though I knew you didn't owe me anything. Despite my...earlier statement. I'm sor—"

"Do not apologize to me again," he growls, leaning closer.

"Sorry. No, I mean, um, sorry for the sorry. Shit." I wince as he chuckles.

"Nervous, little witch?"

Without a thought, my tongue flicks out and brushes against his bottom lip. He groans, the sound rumbling from deep within him. He seals his mouth to mine, and my mind goes blank. It's like I'm floating outside my body, gazing down at the scene spread out. My back against the bricks, him leaning into me, the sun beating down on us, my flushed cheeks and my eyes closed.

I snap back into my body, and butterflies erupt in my belly. My chest tightens and my hands end up clinging to his shoulders. His own hand grasps the back of my neck, and he tugs me closer. He breaks off the kiss and rests his forehead against mine.

"Say something," he breathes.

"Why'd you stop?"

He grins, then pulls away. I let out a shriek when he tips me over his shoulder. His large hand wraps around my thigh and his long strides eat up the distance to my front door, which he kicks closed behind us. Shadows chase us down the hallway, and I bite my lip to contain my smile.

My breath whooshes from me as he drops me onto the bed. His wings snap out, the claws on the tips curling, then disappearing. His shadows blend together, forming tendrils that reach for me. My heels slip on the sheets as I scramble backward. He grabs my ankle and drags me toward him. A giggle bursts from me until he drops to his knees.

His long fingers wrap around my calves, the heat seeping through my leggings. His dark eyes find mine, twin flames flickering in their depths. When he leans forward, my breath hitches. With my knees bent over the edge of the mattress, he's perfectly placed to fit himself between my legs. My mouth waters and my mind spins off into a thousand different possibilities. I can't read him, though. I have no idea what he's planning.

His palms slide up to my hips, and he rests his chin on my stomach. "I need you to talk to me."

"What?" I rasp, struggling to keep my eyes on him while not giving myself a double chin. Thankfully, he tugs me upright and kneels between my legs.

He sighs, the flames winking out in his eyes. "It's been less than an hour for me. For you? It's been six months. Then I waltz back in and we find ourselves here after a few minutes. I don't want you like this."

Pain lances through my chest and I attempt to keep the hurt from my face. I tuck my chin to my chest and my hair slips over my shoulder. Another rejection wasn't on my to-do list for the day.

In my weak moments, I wondered what I would do if he came back. The possibilities ranged from cussing him out to jumping his bones and everything in between. I thought if we got to this point...I don't know. Maybe I could turn my brain off and not worry about our uncertain future. Or we'd be so caught up in the moment. I didn't expect him to reject me as soon as we got going.

"Clara?" Omen whispers, tucking his knuckle under my chin and forces my gaze to his. "I need to know you're not making a rash decision."

I let out a sharp laugh. "This is the most thought-out and yet rash decision I've ever made in my life."

His brows pull low. "I don't know what that means, which isn't surprising."

"Because you're a demon?"

"And because you're a witch." His fingers dig into my thighs and desire ignites within me once more.

"Is that supposed to scare me off? You want me to send you away and paint over the summoning circle? Might make things easier." I narrow my eyes, watching for his reaction. I don't really want to do any of that. I just want him to pick me.

I've waited for six months for him. Despite what I told him—what I told myself—I never stopped searching for him. Every room I stepped into. Every morning when I opened my eyes. Every time the book dropped onto the counter. Over and over, that damn book would tumble open, revealing spells revolving around demons. Between summoning circles, binding spells, and truth serums, all involving demons, I was about to bury it in the woods. It would just find its way back to me, though.

Regardless, the damned thing kept following me around, showing up in the most unlikely places. I took it as a sign not to get rid of the summoning circle. I've been waiting for the payment, though. Magic will come for me one way or another. I wonder if the cost rose each time I called Omen to this world. Who's paying for my choices?

"Clara," he growls, and I snap my attention back to him.

"What happened when you left?" I ask. Omen has to be the one paying the price. There's no one else close to me unless the magic would pick one of my friends, but I barely speak to them these days other than a text to check in once every three weeks.

Omen scowls and his wings flicker in and out of existence. "Doesn't matter. It wasn't that long for me."

"But your magic. Did it freak out? Were you hurt? Did something happen?" My chest tightens as I wait for his answer. No matter what happened to him, it was because of me. I did it to him without a second thought.

Flames flicker in his dark eyes and his skin takes on a dark hue. "What's this about, little witch?"

"I used the book," I whisper.

The corner of his mouth tips up. "And you think I'm the one who pays? Doubt it. There are very few circumstances where a demon would pay the price for…"

His gaze narrows, then takes on a faraway look. This is about the time he'll keep shit from me. He'll tell me not to worry about it or distract me. Or maybe he'll just poof out of existence again. He seems to do that when things go sideways. I clear my throat and his gaze snaps back to me.

"What circumstances?" I demand.

He shakes his head. "Mostly when there's an agreement in place. Times of war and all that."

He slides his hands to my waist, then up my sides before settling on my cheeks. My brain short circuits as the yearning from minutes ago hits me. He pushes up, still on his knees, and I exhale sharply. Even with me on the bed, he's much taller than me. My mind races, desperately trying to convince myself the height won't be a problem if I'm lying down. Which is ridiculous since I don't know if we'll ever get there.

He leans in, his breath brushing my ear and my stomach flips. "The only way this works is if you submit to me, little witch. The magic flowing through your veins will rise up to protect you if you're not absolutely certain you want this."

I close my eyes, hiding in the comfort of the dark. "I wanted this months ago."

"When?" he whispers, then presses his lips to the sensitive spot behind my ear. "When I was gone?"

He feathers kisses down my neck, making it hard to remember the question. I jolt and my eyes fly open when something touches my waist. Wispy shadows make their way to my inner thighs, then back to my knees. A whimper leaves me when he pushes them apart and he settles between my legs.

"Answer the question, Clara," he murmurs, then sinks his teeth into the soft skin.

"Batteries," I gasp, tipping my head back.

Omen chuckles, though I doubt he understands. It feels like a lifetime ago he changed the batteries in my smoke detector. He probably doesn't remember. I do. I remember everything about him. From the first time he swirled into a poorly drawn summoning circle to now as he nibbles on my earlobe. I stored it all away in the deepest parts of me, hoping for the day he'd see me as something more than just another witch.

His hands slide to my shoulders while his shadows sneak under my shirt. I haven't given much thought to how they work. His shadows come and go, seemingly on a whim. He only touched on the basics when we talked. Now, they feel like an extra set of hands working my body into a frenzy. I can't quite keep up with the sensations. I'm being pulled in so many different directions, never quite able to focus on all the things he's doing to my body.

"What do you want, Clara?" he murmurs, both his hands and shadows pausing in their quest to map my skin.

"You," I breathe, tipping my head back. "All of you."

He growls in response and pushes me down, then covers my body with his. He renews his efforts to find every sensitive spot. His fingers brush my sides, making me shudder. I run my hands up his chest, then hook them behind his head. His lips melt into mine and I lose myself in his kiss.

Whatever happens after, at least I'll have this. I've spent my entire life toeing the line of being a good witch. I did my spell-work and attended coven meetings and followed the rules. Until I didn't. Until I decided to use a book I wasn't supposed to use. And summon a demon I wasn't supposed to summon. And form a connection I wasn't supposed to form.

I rip my mouth away, gasping for air. It's like he's stolen it from my lungs—my being, my soul, my very essence. Doesn't matter since I don't need to breathe. He'll be my sustenance. At least for now.

He kisses his way down my neck. There's a snap and my shirt disappears. I wonder whether he sent it into a void or my laundry basket. The thought vanishes under his touch. My mind empties as I run my hands up his sides, his shirt bunching as I do. The sharp tang of sulfur wafts past my nose and suddenly there's warm skin under my fingers.

I dig my nails into his dark flesh, and he seizes my wrists with his shadows. My arms end up over my head and a giggle spills from me. He growls and I notice the half-moon indents I left behind. They glow a deep orange as if the fire burning within him wants to escape. The marks dissolve slowly until only smooth obsidian skin remains.

"Do it again," he demands huskily.

He grinds his hips into me and I whimper. His hold on my wrists doesn't loosen, making it impossible for me to obey his command.

"Omen," I whine, yanking once more, and he chuckles.

"Something you need, little witch?"

I wiggle underneath him and he drops his lower half, pinning me in place. "If you keep teasing me…"

He snickers and his wings descend over us. I wrap my legs around his waist, desperately trying to get closer. The spark he's ignited inside me flares to life, my desire fanning the flames until I'm stuck in an inferno. He drags his fingertips along my flesh and my eyes flutter closed.

Omen murmurs something I can't quite hear. My whimpers drown out his words. It doesn't really matter. His touch is more than enough. He's driving me to the brink of oblivion and we don't even have our pants off yet.

I gasp when his lips wrap around my nipple and his tongue flicks the hardening bud. I spear my fingers into his hair when he switches to the other one. Horns form under my hands and I grip them tightly. He tries to pull away and I arch into his mouth. His chuckle rumbles through my chest.

"Greedy little witch, I see," he murmurs.

I force his head back and narrow my gaze. "I've waited long enough for this. Stop. Teasing. Me."

A single eyebrow pops up, and he licks his lips. "But I'm having so much fun. Have you been fantasizing about me?" The horns disappear from my hands. "Have you been dreaming about my cock?"

"You have a dirty mouth," I wheeze.

His shadow fingers slide up my body, and I track their progress until I lose sight. They wrap around my throat. I may not be able to see them, but I can feel their warmth. Tiny licks of heat emanate from them, forcing a low moan from me.

"I'm a demon. There are plenty of dirty things I can do with my mouth."

He makes good on his words, nipping his way down my body until he reaches my stomach. I lift my hips, silently begging him to do something, *anything*. He plays with the waistband, tucking a claw underneath and skimming across my skin. It wouldn't take much to slice clean through the material. My bottom lip slips between my teeth as I fixate on his movements.

His black eyes flash red and the material rips away from my body. More of his shadows brush my leggings away, leaving me bare underneath him. His own pants vanish, and I lick my lips.

I've spent the last six months with his cock starring in my dreams. The bars piercing through the top and wrapping around the shaft must have hurt. Maybe they're made of his magical shadows. Except they look hard. The thought has a giggle catching in my throat.

I reach out and run my finger along the metal by his tip. He sucks in a sharp breath and I smirk.

"Careful, witch. You're playing with fire. Literally."

"I'm not afraid of getting burned."

He snorts and I swear flames wick across his chest. One hand grips my waist and the other runs up my thigh. His gaze bores into mine and I swallow hard. I jolt when he swipes a finger between my legs and gathers the wetness. My eyes flutter shut as he strokes me into a frenzy. I'm not used to someone worshiping me the way he is.

He buries his face into my neck as his tip nudges against me. He slips in and I gasp, my back arching. Every time he touches me, I feel something stronger—deeper—somewhere in my soul. Everything is heightened beyond what I'm used to. It has to be because he's a demon. He brings out a side of me I didn't realize. My pleasure builds as his hands, his shadows, and his mouth glide across my skin. His length slips deeper and a moan echoes around us and I realize it's coming from me.

I dig my heels into his lower back, desperate to pull him

closer. He rests his forehead against mine, twin flames flickering in his eyes.

"Please," I whisper.

His low growl resonates through the air as he thrusts into me. My mouth parts and he seals our lips together. Every single bar sends shockwaves through my body as he pulls out slowly. Already I'm on the brink of an orgasm. I lock my ankles, and he surges into me once more.

He whispers against my lips, but I can't hear him over the roaring in my ears. Shadows swirl around us and stars burst within them. A shudder rolls through me when one of his piercings rubs against my clit. Ecstasy blooms within me, and flames lick through my veins as I tumble into oblivion.

Omen whispers words of encouragement in my ear as he slams into me, prolonging the sensations rolling through me. He pushes upright and his feet slam onto the floorboards. My legs fall from his waist, but he grips my hips, keeping me in place. I follow his gaze, which is locked on where we're joined. Another orgasm rises as I watch his cock disappearing into me.

I crash over the edge once more and swim through the euphoria. His shadows explode out of him and envelop us until all I make out is his red eyes blinking from the sudden darkness. It's so like the first time I met him, I jolt and squeeze around his cock. He groans, my name on his lips. Not little witch or some other pet name. *Clara* falls from him like I'm his salvation from damnation, his light in the dark, his solace among the nightmares.

A tendril of smoke reaches for me and brushes against my skin, heating me from the inside out. Whether this is his magic or something else, I don't know. Nevertheless, it links us together, solidifying into more than mere mist and shadows. I close my eyes, finally feeling at peace.

CHAPTER SIXTEEN
OMEN

I cross my arms as I stare at the summoning circle. Clara wasn't messing around when she said she sealed this thing. There's a sheen to the floor, preserving not only the chalk marks, but the scuffs littering the wood as well.

As my gaze brushes over the marks, I try to decipher where they came from. A scratch here, a gouge there. Some of them could have come from me. In the beginning, I wasn't very careful about my claws. They may be formed from shadows, but they're capable of a lot more than most would expect. More substantial than smoke, yet less than my actual claws. To someone like Clara, they're as solid as I want them to be. To myself, they're an echo of a sensation, more magic than physical touch.

A heavy sigh falls from my lips, and I drop my arms. I shouldn't be here. I *should* be tucked next to Clara with her in my arms. If she wakes up and I'm gone, she'll probably think the worst. Ever since the birds started chirping two hours ago, though, I've been thinking about this damn circle. Questions piled up until I couldn't take it anymore, and here I am.

"Omen?" Clara's sleepy voice washes over me, and an unbidden smile creeps over my face.

I hold out my arm and she slips underneath, tucking her body close to mine. The large black shirt she's wearing rides up her thighs, and I slip my hand underneath the fabric. I revel in the feel of her soft skin under my palm.

"You should be sleeping still," I murmur.

She yawns, then rubs the tip of her nose on my chest. "I had to pee."

"Charming, little witch," I say softly, and she snorts.

"What are you doing?"

"Trying to figure out how Dimitri got here. Him being here isn't a big deal, but if someone else shows up...well, I can't guarantee they'll be friendly."

She pulls back and gazes up at me. "Uh, Dimitri being here wasn't a big deal? Is that what we're going with? Because you practically threw him through a wall and then ordered me around in my own house."

I roll my eyes, tugging her close once more. "I didn't say I handled it well. It just wasn't as big of a deal as I made it out to be. I wasn't thinking clearly." I clear my throat. "However, the circle opened up an avenue through the void. Except it should have contained him here. Instead, he popped right into your bedroom."

"And you're trying to figure out why?"

"Mhm." I release her and drop into a crouch. My fingers brush over the lacquered surface. I let out a soft *oh* and snicker.

Clara drops next to me. "What? Did I do something wrong?"

"Just your shitty chalk work, little witch." I point to my sigil. "See this line? It trails off at the curl like you dragged the chalk along instead of picking it up. This allowed for others to channel the energy flowing from one dimension to another."

She tilts her head this way and that before huffing. "Well, shit. How do we fix it?"

I sigh and push to my feet. "Can't. Nothing we can do."

I pivot and saunter into the kitchen. Clara stumbles after me as I fill the kettle for tea. She collapses onto the stool and I wonder if I could get her to go back to bed. We spent most of the day yesterday testing the limits of her bed frame. Then the floor. And the shower, though that last one didn't quite work out. Not being able to control my shadows didn't help. They kept knocking open the shower door, spraying water everywhere. It may have ended in laughter, but she needs a better shower if she wants to live out that particular fantasy.

She sighs as I set a steaming cup in front of her. "What do you mean, there's nothing we can do? I thought if I sealed it—I didn't mean to fuck it up."

"You didn't fuck it up, Clara." I lean against the counter, then straighten again when she lets out a giggle.

"My kitchen isn't exactly made for demons. I'd apologize, but I don't much feel like it." Her snarkiness is broken by a yawn. "So, do I have to worry about random demons popping in? Because that could be disconcerting, to say the least."

"I suppose it would be. Demons aren't being summoned often, though. Still doesn't make sense why Dimitri just showed up. Maybe you should get rid of the summoning circle," I murmur.

Her head snaps up. "But that means you wouldn't be able to come back. Unless that's a subtle hint that you got what you wanted—"

My shadows snap out and cover her mouth, cutting off her bullshit. "Would you like to try again?"

Her eyes narrow, then she nods, and I pull my shadows back. "You said if I got rid of the circle, then no one could come. So, if you want me to get rid of it, stands to reason you don't want to come back."

I don't know how to explain to her what's going on in my head. My arguments are selfish and personal. Influencing her either way won't help in the long run. And if she gets hurt because I encouraged her to keep the circle, I'll never forgive myself. Even if I don't plan on binding my soul to hers, I wouldn't be able to live with myself after that.

"I can't have an opinion on it, Clara. I'll have to live with your

decision either way," I finally say when her gaze becomes too insistent.

I lean against the counter and sip my tea, feigning indifference while my emotions rage inside. From the look on her face, I'm not doing a very good job.

"Well, you're not very helpful, are you?"

"What would you have me say?"

"I don't know, maybe what you want?"

"You." I take another sip.

Her nostrils flare. "You mean my pussy."

Slowly, I shake my head. We're tiptoeing into dangerous territory.

"Oh, so the sex was bad?"

I rear back, almost knocking my head on the cupboard. "What? That's not what I said."

"It was implied," she says haughtily. She sips her tea as if she didn't just throw a bomb in my face.

"Not going to work, little witch." I set my cup down and saunter around the island. She turns with me until her back is pressed against the counter. "Distracting me isn't going to make the conversation go away."

"Can you blame a witch? I mean, you're essentially making me choose how this goes with absolutely no input from you."

I lean my hands on the island, boxing her in. A shiver rolls through her body and my cock hardens. As much as I want to spread her on the counter and bury my face between her legs, she needs to make a decision. Then I can reward her.

"I can't help you, Clara. You have to figure out if the risks are worth it."

"The risk of some rando popping into the summoning circle without me knowing."

"Among other things."

Her head snaps up at that, a wild look in her eyes. "What other things?"

I slide my hand to the back of her neck and squeeze, then let

her go and straighten. "I don't know how long I can go back and forth without...difficulties. I have responsibilities in Hell. With time not lining up in this dimension, I have no idea how long I'll be gone in either place. You'd be living—"

"The life I choose. Whichever way I go."

"Exactly. Whatever you choose, you'll have to live with the outcome."

She traces a finger down my chest, over my stomach, and hooks onto my boxer briefs. "Why do demons wear clothes? Seems like they'd just go around naked."

"Same reason humans do, I suppose. Is this your subtle way of trying to get me naked?"

She smirks, toying with the fabric. "Maybe. I might need a little refresher of what I'd be missing."

I scan the island, then grab her wrist and push it away. My waistband snaps into my stomach and she grins. I slip my hands to her waist and lift her. Her ass hits the cold counter and she squeals. I nudge her knees apart, making room to step between her legs. She freezes, gazing up at me with wide eyes.

"This is my shirt, you know," I murmur.

"Did you want it back?"

"You're going to need it for a bit. Unless you'd like to be naked on a cold counter."

"If you're doing it right, I won't be cold for long."

I lean into her, our lips brushing and whisper, "Is that a challenge, little witch?"

I seal our mouths together before she can answer. She moans, her hands sliding up my chest. Her nails dig into my skin and I groan. My tongue sweeps along hers, devouring her—relishing her taste. When her heels hook around my thighs, I pull away and rest my forehead on hers.

She sucks in a sharp breath when I guide her down onto the island. She lifts her hips and I tug her underwear off. I skim my palms from her ankles to her thighs. Leaning over her, I move my hands to her tits and the shirt rides up. A lifetime could pass and I would still be capitvated by the sight of her. She grabs my wrists and I brush my thumbs over her nipples. They turn into hard nubs, and I lick my lips.

"Omen, please," she breathes, and I stop, earning myself a glare.

"You need to make a decision about the circle, Clara."

Should I be doing this while I'm playing with her body? Probably not. The more I think about it, the less I care. I can't keep my hands off her now that I've had a taste of her. Now that I know what she sounds like when I'm deep inside her, there's an urgency within me. Going another minute without hearing it again would be a special type of torture.

A low whine leaves her as she digs her heels into my thighs. "After. I need..."

"I know what you want, but you *need* to tell me what you plan to do." I pinch her nipple to accent my point.

"I can't just decide on a whim," she whimpers as I roll the hard nub between my fingers. I release it when she tips her chin up and stares at the ceiling. "I wish..."

My body covers hers and she sighs, wrapping her arms around my neck. I've never been one to cuddle, yet with Clara I can't get enough. I'm sure it's the thread tying us together. Being connected to someone is new for me. I can't tell Clara about being soulbound. It'll only influence her decision about my staying. Plus, I won't let her throw away her life for an existence in Hell.

It's been hundreds of years since a witch was in Hell. The demons would fucking lose it. There'd be meetings and councils and paperwork. So much fucking paperwork. At least she'd be safe there, but I can't risk her resenting me later.

"What do you wish, little witch?" I murmur into her neck.

"I wish there was a way to get rid of the circle, but keep you," she whispers.

It's a good thing my face is hidden or she'd know I'm keeping things from her. I hum, hoping she lets it go. If she keeps pushing, I'll confess everything, which will freak her out and end with her

banishing me. Neither of us needs to go through something like that. A loud thud echoes through the room and my shadows burst from my body, shielding her from the threat.

Clara laughs, pushing at them as if they'll just dissolve. "You're jumpy for a demon."

The shadows form into wings, and I search the kitchen for the source of the noise. I scowl when I spot the black book lying innocently on the counter next to the stove. If only it would have fallen onto an open flame.

"Do not move," I growl, then push off of her.

I stalk over to the book and go to slam it shut when I catch the spell. Hesitation takes over and I stare at the page. Not a spell, a description. A definition.

"Sorry. I must have put it back wonky." Clara says, and I glance over my shoulder. "What'd it open to?"

I close the book gently, though all I want to do is rip out every single page. I nestle it between two cookbooks, then glare at the tome. I'll have to get rid of it before the damned thing guides her down the path I'm desperately trying to avoid. Keeping information from her probably isn't the best idea. If she finds out, she'll be pissed. I'd deserve whatever bullshit she throws my way at that point.

"Omen?"

I clear my throat, realizing I didn't answer her question. I could lie and make up something, but she might read into whatever spell I throw out. Then we'll be in a whole other mess. Telling the truth isn't an option.

"It was nothing." I round the island again and run my hands up her legs. "Now, where were we?"

CHAPTER SEVENTEEN
CLARA

"Oh no. You're not going to distract me by—oh." A moan slips out and my eyes flutter shut.

I should push him for an answer, but with what his tongue is doing, I can't really be bothered. Pleasure has rendered me useless for conversation. At some point, we'll need to talk about the future. Not now. That'd be weird. Except half my brain is focused on what the book showed him and the other is zeroed in on his long fingers slowly pushing into me.

"So wet for me," he says huskily. "Were you this wet when you were playing with yourself? Were you imagining my fingers instead of your own?"

I whimper, which isn't really an answer. If he's wanting actual words, he's going to have to stop. If he stops, my heel will end up in his throat. I still haven't fully decided whether or not I want him to stay. The fact he finally made a move doesn't quite make up for him not coming back for six months.

After that long, I'd thought I'd banish his ass if he came back. Instead, I let him in with open arms. If he sticks around, we're going to need to talk.

Omen's lips brush mine, and he whispers, "Distracted?"

My eyes snap open and I wince. "Sorry."

His thumb presses into my clit, making me gasp. "Stop apologizing. Get out of your head."

I nod and he hums, holding my gaze as he dips between my legs once more. I focus on his fingers, his tongue, his mouth. When his horns brush my thighs, I press my lips together. They flash in and out of existence as if his magic is running rampant. He tried to explain how it works, but most of it went over my head. His wings flutter like there's a breeze in the middle of my kitchen. The tips brush over my skin, leaving goosebumps in their wake.

He drives his fingers into me harder, faster, while his tongue swirls around my clit. My pleasure builds and my stomach tightens in anticipation. I lose myself in the feelings overriding my senses.

"Don't stop," I chant over and over under my breath as I teeter on the edge of ecstasy. He hums and my legs start to shake.

Just when I'm about to come, he vanishes. He doesn't pull away or slow down. He completely disappears, my orgasm along with him. I let out a frustrated cry and slam my palms on the counter. Glancing down, I'm not surprised to find only my dining room staring back at me.

"Omen," I yell. "I swear if you don't come back and finish what you started..."

Silence greets me. The kind of quiet one feels in their soul. It seeps into me and a numbness spreads through my body. I struggle to breathe and an ache blooms in my chest. It cements me to the hard surface beneath me, keeping me exactly where it wants me. Who *it* is, I don't know and I'm not sure I want to. I snatch at my thoughts, yet they slip away.

I linger in the stillness, lying on my cold island, and wondering how the hell I got myself into this mess. All I wanted was my jar opened. I wasn't looking for a handyman or a friend or a lover. For six months, I've been trying to convince myself his leaving was for the best. We were getting too close. Lines were being blurred.

I was using him as a distraction to cover up my feelings about

my friends. Once I figured it out, I reached out to them. My olive branch didn't do much at repairing anything, but I didn't feel bad about the situation anymore. We're at different points in our lives and that's okay. At least, that's what I've been telling myself. I'd finally gotten to a place where I was ready to move on. I've mourned the loss of their companionship and found other things to occupy my time.

Finally, I was starting to feel like myself. I filled my time with renovations, work, and hobbies. Cooking, crocheting, drawing, and gardening. They've all helped in some way, but they didn't fill the hole in me.

The longer Omen was away, the tighter the thread within me pulled. It anchored him in my mind, not fully allowing me to let him go. It's why I never erased the summoning circle. It's why I lacquered over the chalk, etching it into the wood.

"What good is a summoning circle if the damn demon doesn't show up when you call him?" I huff and slip off the counter. "Omen!"

I hold my breath as I scan the space. Nothing moves. No one appears. I exhale heavily and wait for a whole minute. It doesn't make a difference. What if something happened? What if he's in trouble? I wouldn't imagine he'd leave voluntarily, especially when he was seconds away from making me come. Based on last night, he was hyperfocused on sending me into oblivion.

I press my lips together and grimace. "Dimitri?"

Calling Omen's friend might not be the best idea, but he'd be the best demon to ask whether or not Omen is in trouble. The longer I wait, the more my anxiety takes hold of me. I jolt and knock my back into the counter when a loud thump ricochets around me. I stumble to the book lying innocently next to the oven.

"Why the hell would I need the summoning circle? I already have one." I flip the book closed and sigh before turning away. Papers shuffle behind me and I sigh.

I stare at the text, trying to decipher what I'm missing. I jump backward with a squeak when the pages flip. When it settles, I lean closer.

"You've got to be fucking kidding me. Like I'd travel to Hell just to go after my...demon. Who would do that?"

I scoop up the book and read it again. My feet move before I've fully decided to follow the directions. I'd be a fool of a witch to do this, especially since I have no idea where Omen is. It's not like I'd just drop in front of him. I'd probably end up wandering around pits of fire. Then I'd be stuck in another dimension and no one would know where I was. Maybe that wouldn't be so bad.

Once I step into my spell room, a cold draft hits me, and I shiver. I drop the book and scowl at the swirly script. Still, I end up gathering the black candles and hemlock. Because of course the spell calls for hemlock. I'm surprised it doesn't require belladonna.

Skimming the text again, I let out a breathless laugh. "Of course I need belladonna to get back. Like hell I'm drinking any of this shit."

I dump my goods on the ground and start setting up the candles. I'm a lot more careful this time around. Once I toss the hemlock in the center, I send a silent plea to my mother to guide me.

Flame flicks from the match and I hold my breath as I light each one. I could use my own magic, but I'm terrified of messing this up. When I glance back at the book, I swallow hard. Instead of the creamy pages, they've turned black. The calligraphy no longer flows seamlessly from one word to the next. Now it's a harsh scrawl laid out in red.

"Fucking Latin," I growl, running my finger along the words. "Why can't you just translate yourself for fuck's sake?"

I yelp and yank my hand away when the text swims on the page and translates into English. I should have given this thing to Omen. He could have thrown it into one of those fiery pits down

there. It probably would show up again since it's cursed. Except I wouldn't know Omen if I hadn't opened the thing.

"If you fuck me over, I'll destroy you," I whisper as I glare at the dark pages. Then I realize I'm threatening a book. I'm just stalling at this point.

I stumble through the first few sentences, then clear my throat and start again. I gather the book to my chest and stare at the circle flickering in the candlelight. Nothing moves, though there's an energy in the air. Waiting isn't easy. All I want to do is jump into the middle and deal with the consequences. Or run as far away as possible. Except I can't leave Omen in trouble.

"Except he probably isn't in trouble. Shit," I mumble.

Nothing good can come from a trip to Hell. What a ridiculous notion. I blame the lack of an orgasm for losing my head. If I would have just thought things through, I wouldn't be in here with candles and hemlock.

I cling to the book as I blow out the candles one by one. I leave the plant where it is, making a note to clean it up later. My chest tightens as I turn toward the door, then immediately spin back. Omen's cat meows from the center of the circle.

"Seriously, Handsome? Get out of there."

He tilts his head, which freaks me out every time. It's like he's mimicking human behaviors—particularly Omen's. He's clearly not a cat from this realm. He meows again, then picks up his front paw and licks at his fur. For such an ugly cat with his smashed face, he's pretty adorable. I still can't get over how tiny he is, though it's hard to tell with all the fluff.

"Handsome," I snap, and he blinks lazily at me, then continues his bath. "Let's go get a treat."

I tuck the book under my arm and edge closer to the circle. Who knows what would happen if I stepped inside. I crouch and hold out my hand as if I'll be able to coax him to me. He twitches and I swear flames flicker in his eyes. A millisecond later and they're gone, replaced by the regular green glow. He glances at his feet, then ducks his head to the hemlock. The candles flare to life and I gasp.

"No, Handsome." I tumble into the summoning circle. The book slams to the ground, and the cat ends up in my arms.

There's a tug in my gut and the room disappears.

CHAPTER EIGHTEEN
OMEN

I pace across the small area—a cage really. I don't know what the fuck is going on and no one seems to have answers. Dimitri shuffles in his sleep. Is he considered asleep if he's actually unconscious? At least he's still breathing. I resist the urge to kick him.

It's his fault I'm here. His fault I was ripped away from Clara. His fault I have a raging hard on. I shake my head and shove the last thought away. He definitely didn't get me hard. Clara, on the other hand...

I slam my fists into the bars and snarl. I haven't even talked to anyone. When I was yanked away from my little witch, I could have burned entire dimensions to the ground. Anyone who came near me would have felt my wrath. Yet all I was met with was a cell and Dimitri. I couldn't very well take him out. He's clearly as much a victim as me.

None of which matters since I'm still stuck in here. I have no idea how long I've been gone, nor how long I've been in here. Down here there's only a blue hue to everything. I can't even pinpoint where in Hell I am.

"Omen?" Dimitri croaks out, and I grit my teeth.

"Start talking, Dimitri." I try to keep my voice even. Taking out my rage on him won't help either of us.

"Uh, welcome to the cage?"

I snort, shaking my head as I stare into the darkness. "What a clever name. Who thought that one up?"

"Triton, of course. He sent me down here to get someone. Then I got that weird tingly feeling again, and *bam*, I was in a closet. Spent a couple minutes in there, too terrified to come out on account of what happened last time I was in a random person's house, which wasn't so random seeing as how it was your—"

"Get to the point," I growl. The last thing I need is him calling Clara my girlfriend, or worse, my soulbound.

"Okay, touchy. After that, I felt the tug again, and *bam*, I was in here. 'Cept now the door was locked and I was on the other side of it. Don't know what happened, but I've just been waiting for someone to come get me. I thought it'd be quick."

I finally turn to face him. "How long have you been down here?"

He shrugs. "Don't know. I keep getting pulled back to the human realm. It was disorienting. I'd come back and eventually I couldn't handle the magical trip. I'd pass out, come to, get shoved into limbo—"

"I get it. You don't have to overexplain everything Dimitri," I say, exhaustion lining my voice. He gives me an apologetic look, then pushes to his feet. "You know I didn't mean—"

"I know. Forget sometimes. Mind going a mile a minute. Sometimes it's hard to slow down. Take out the unimportant bits. You know," he mutters.

"I do. So knock it the fuck off. How did I get down here?"

He shrugs again, and I suck in a sharp breath. He's being absolutely no help. Usually, it's nice he's distracted by the next shiny object and doesn't think too deeply into things. He's excellent at listening and gives solid advice when he's locked in. He just won't pry if I don't tell him to. Unless he gets a bug up his butt and hyperfixates on my problems instead of his own. Not that Clara is a problem. Just the thought of her has my lungs seizing, and I brace my hands on my knees.

"Maybe you should flame out. See if that pops the lock or

something." He leans against the wall, exhaustion etched in every line of his body.

"You could have shocked the shit out of it."

He holds up his hand and a soft glow weaves through his fingers, pulsating with his heartbeat. It's nothing like his usual energy. While it's beautiful for a quiet night by the fire, it's not what we need to get us out of here. The soft flickers will be perfect the next time he's trying to get laid. Too bad the door isn't susceptible to his charms.

"Pretty, but not particularly useful," I say.

"Careful or I'll steal your girl." He smirks as he drops his hand. "Too soon?"

I huff, turning back to the darkness. "Be glad she's not here or we'd have more trouble than we can handle."

A soft meow echoes through the space and I groan. Dimitri lets out an *aww,* and when I turn around, he's scratching Clara's cat. How the little fucker got down here, I have no idea. I'm not surprised, though.

"Look how cute she is," Dimitri coos.

"Fuck me," I breathe, planting my fists on my hips and tucking my chin to my chest.

"Shit. Omen? I think she's hurt."

My head snaps up and I rush toward them. No matter how much I want to drop-kick the feline into the sun, I can't let it die on me. Clara seems to love this thing. I never got to ask her if he was her familiar, though Dimitri mentioned the practice fell off a few centuries ago.

Still, Clara isn't your typical witch. From what I've seen, she dabbles in the old arts more often than not, what with that damn book she uses. Even if Sunshine isn't her familiar, he's definitely important to her. She'd be devastated if something happened to him.

I drop to my knees, and the cat gazes at me over his shoulder. His dark squished face looks exactly the same. He's not favoring any of his limbs and there's no blood that I can see.

"Where?" I snarl as I run my hands through his fur.

"She looks like she ran into something. Cat's faces aren't supposed to look like that."

I heave out a sigh, tipping my head back. "First of all, it's a he. Second, that's just his face. I think Clara rescued it or something."

Dimitri snorts and gathers the cat up in his arms. "Let me get this straight, your little witch has a cat, which probably is a familiar—"

"Or she rescued it."

He plows on, ignoring my interruption. "You're freaking out about it being hurt, but you hate cats. And you're still clinging to the fact you don't care about Clara?"

I scowl, glancing away. "I never said I didn't care for her. I'm just acutely aware of the risks of getting involved with a witch."

"Uh, Omen?"

"None of which has anything to do with her personally. A witch doesn't belong in Hell. If she'd just get rid of the summoning circle...fuck, if she never chalked it in the first place, we wouldn't be in this mess."

A soft sigh behind me has me closing my eyes. Of course, she followed her damn cat all the way to the depths of Hell. Because why not? I'm not even surprised she popped up right when I was talking shit. It's not like I have any luck to speak of whatsoever. To be fair, very little of my rant had anything to do with her.

She's not to blame. She just wanted to have a jar opened. I could have told her to get rid of the circle or left as soon as she called for me the next time. I could have stayed away or kept my walls up around her.

Except I know I wouldn't have been able to resist her. Not with our souls being bound to one another. We were always destined to meet. I didn't have to weave our lives together, though. And now I've fucked it up before I've really explored where our future could lead.

If I don't turn around, I won't have to face her. Maybe she'll just poof out and forget everything in the void. From Dimitri's grimace, I doubt Fortune is on my side. He's a fickle creature, much like Karma. For as similar as they are, they bicker like the siblings they are, rarely teaming up. I'd be content to never cross either one of their paths again. Not that Karma leaves anyone alone.

"Omen," Dimitri hisses, and I snap back to reality.

"Sorry," Clara says softly. "I didn't mean to interrupt. Actually, I didn't really think this would...I decided against..." She huffs, then clears her throat. "Your cat was about to eat hemlock. I stopped him and the summoning circle sent me here. If someone could just point me to the nearest portal, I'll be out of your hair."

Dimitri clutches the cat closer to his chest, and I roll my eyes. I push to my feet and snatch the feline from him despite his protests. I'm not letting him keep her pet. When I finally face her, she's avoiding my gaze. I don't blame her. I shove Handsome or Sunshine or whatever the hell she calls him, through the bars and wait.

Her nostrils flare. "I'm not taking the cat, Omen."

"I'll take him," Dimitri calls, and a flash of heat bursts from the top of my head. "Or not."

"Well, I sure as shit ain't taking him. He's yours."

She shakes her head, pressing her lips together. I pull the cat back and twist around to drop him into Dimitri's lap. I'm not about to argue with her about a fucking pet while I'm locked in a cage.

"Can you find a key?" I ask as I turn back to her.

"So, you are in trouble?"

"Trouble? Not really. Energy is probably just off or the magic. Either way, we're stuck in here."

She nods, staring at the lock. She steps closer and a shiver runs through my body when I finally get a good look at her. Dimitri better be absorbed with her cat instead of staring at Clara's bare legs. Not much time must have passed between my leaving and her coming. I wince and my cock hardens. I'm sure she was pissed when I left her on the edge of an orgasm. Makes two of us.

Metal clanks and the door swings toward her. She gives me a look as she wiggles the handle up and down. My mouth drops open and Dimitri cackles from behind me. I spin around, intent on sending his ass to a random pocket dimension for a time-out. Bastard could have opened the damn thing this entire time. Not that I was much better, but it's easier to blame him.

"Well shit," Dimitri wheezes, and the cat jumps from his arms, giving him an affronted look. Shock flashes on his face and he disappears, leaving an undercurrent of electricity humming through the air.

"Does he do that often? Or is it me?"

"He doesn't, or rather, he didn't, but I don't think it has anything to do with you." I step out of the cage, and she stumbles back. "You want to tell me how you got down here?"

She wrings her hands together. "Well, you disappeared. I got pissed, then I got freaked out. I may have thought I could use the summoning circle, but I thought better of it. Except Handsome popped in and I thought he was going to eat the hemlock. I ended up in the circle and—"

"You used the book, didn't you?" I growl, crossing my arms, and she nods. "Well, fuck."

She presses her hands to her stomach and her face tightens. Almost as if she's in pain. "Can you send me back?"

"Can I send you back alone? No. If you..." I tilt my head as she grimaces, then jump forward as she crumples. I catch her before she hits the ground and gather her to my chest.

"Sorry," she whispers. Her body shivers uncontrollably in my grasp, and I clutch her tighter.

"Oh, little witch. What have you done?"

CHAPTER NINETEEN
CLARA

"Cold," I whine, my teeth chattering.

Darkness swirls around us and my ears pop. Nothingness presses into me and I blink, desperately searching for a pinprick of light in this void. When I close my eyes, images flash against my lids, too quickly for me to decipher. Numbness spreads through my limbs until I can't feel Omen's arms around me anymore. I open my mouth to call for him, but no sound comes out.

For some reason, my brain doesn't freak out. Other than the chill seeping into my muscles, I feel nothing. It's like my body has disappeared, leaving only the essence of feeling behind.

Slowly, a light comes into view, growing larger the closer I get. Or maybe it's moving and I'm staying still. I'm sure I'll wonder about it later if I remember this. I stare into the brightness as it widens, almost like a movie theater screen.

Omen's wings come into view and he glances over his shoulder. Orange glows around his frame, and I squint to make out what's behind him. A grin takes over his face, and my heart clenches. He takes off, the muscles in his back rippling. The scene fills out and flames come into focus.

Omen runs over a rickety bridge, dodging fireballs. Panic plucks at my psyche as he jumps from one wooden pillar with a disk on top. His wings vanish, reappearing in the form of a thin tail with a tuft of shadows at the end. He lands on a small plat-form and sparks fly from his bare feet.

The scene dissolves and materializes into another one. Omen stands at the edge of a cliff, magma flowing at the bottom of the chasm. Every so often, a lick of fire erupts from the surface. He gazes at the oozing liquid, then at the opposite ridge. The view hurtles into the air, making my stomach roll, until it finally settles with me peering at him from above. His muscles bunch, and I realize what he's going to do a second before it becomes reality. I open my mouth to scream, yet nothing comes out.

He launches himself into the emptiness, his arms pinwheel-ing. I wish I could look away. I don't want to watch him die. With no perceivable eyes, I'm forced to witness his demise. And then I'll be stuck in this in-between space. Alone and mourning the demon I shouldn't have wanted in the first place. Maybe I'll be forced to relive this moment again and again in some sick punish-ment for not knowing my place in the world.

To my utter amazement, he lands on the other side safely. He tips his head back, grinning into the darkness, and something within me blooms to life. The numbness seeps from me bit by bit.

Omen makes it all of one step before a thin rope made of pure flame lashes from the crevice and wraps around his ankle. A scream erupts from me as it yanks him off his feet and drags him toward the edge. His fingers scramble for purchase, claws digging into the rocky ground. Wings sprout from his back once more and thrash through the air.

Tears spring to my eyes and slide down my cheeks, though I have no hands to wipe them away. As my vision blurs, he slips over the edge and his roar splits the night.

Darkness envelops me and I slip into a stupor. Emotions mean nothing, my body has disappeared again, and I no longer remember why there's a deep despair resting in my soul. It doesn't matter here in the void, anyway.

Gradually, I recognize my fingers clutching something soft, arms cradling me close, and the smell of sulfur and cinnamon.

Wherever I was and whatever I was doing doesn't matter as much as the chill snaking down my spine and the spasms making my muscles twitch. It's too dark to see anything, but at least I'm no longer floating in a sea of blackness.

When the shadows dissipate, we're in a large bedroom. If I wasn't getting smothered from the inside out, I'd admire the dark walls and the ginormous bed. At least I get to enjoy the fluffiness of the covers when he sets me on it. I wish I could savor how comfortable it is. I roll on my side and curl into a ball. It's not like the cramps I had before. It's an ache attacking my bones and stretching my tendons to the breaking point.

A choked sob leaves me as I press harder into Omen. I scoot closer as he kneels on the bed, trying to soak up his warmth. He brings his other hand to my face, and my eyes flutter closed. It won't do much for long. Even now, there's less heat coming from him.

He's probably not equipped to deal with something like this. Taking care of a human while they're sick probably isn't something he's done before. When I had cramps, he clearly didn't know what he was doing. If this sickness is witchy work at play, a demon would stay far away. Except he brought me here.

I whimper and I realize I've sucked all the warmth from his palms. When he pulls them away, I inhale sharply and my eyes flash open.

"I'm sorry. You can take me back." I groan and bury my face in his pillow.

"Clara," he says sharply, but I don't move. "Tell me what you did."

"Nothing," I wheeze as a bolt of pain lances through my lungs, making every breath hurt. "I didn't *do* anything. I'm fine. I didn't summon you. I just used it to get to Hell."

He sighs, running his fingers through his hair as he sits back against the headboard. They tangle with his horns, and he drops his hand to his side. I don't know what else to tell him. It was just a spell—no better or worse than the others. I haven't used anything other than the summoning circle spell, so I assumed this one wouldn't screw me over.

I roll to my back and yelp as something sharp pokes my hip. Omen practically dives over me and snatches up the book. He growls and drops the heavy tome between us, and it brushes me. A shock zips up my arm and I yank it away. Omen shoves off the bed and glares at the dark cover.

"If the damn thing is going to lash out at me, maybe I'll return the favor. I should have dragged it to the depths of Hell and burned it when I had the chance."

"You can't burn it. Besides, it's an heirloom."

"It's a fucking menace. And it's making you sick," he snarls, still glaring at the black cover.

"It's a book, not a poison. It's not making me sick." My voice breaks and my shoulders shake as chills wrack my body. Tears spring to my eyes, and I close them so he doesn't notice. Maybe it's embarrassment, though that doesn't make sense. He took care of me when I was on my period. He saved me from the washing machine. He's been saving me over and over, regardless of the requests.

He drops his hands on the bed and leans close. "What. Did. You. Do." It's not a request.

"I...I got the book. No, the book fell off the shelf. It opened to the summoning circle, I assume because I was trying to summon you back." I wince as another bolt of pain hits my back.

Omen mutters a curse under his breath. My chin trembles uncontrollably. I don't know if it's the chills razing my body or the memory sitting at the edge of my mind.

A familiar emotion blossoms in my chest, and I realize I've gone too far. Hell was supposed to be scary, terrifying, and full of screaming. At least according to certain people. I wasn't worried about where I was going, I was concerned for Omen, to the point where I fell straight into the depths.

And now I'm here, hoping he won't throw me away, all while telling him I'll leave. It's ridiculous and unhelpful to my situation.

I'm making the same mistakes with him that I made with my friends. Avoidance is apparently my personality. If I pretend it isn't happening, then I can dodge the pain.

I close my eyes and an image floats up from the darkness. It's blurry with a silhouette of a demon with wings spread wide surrounded by shades of grey and red. A hot lance rips into me, but I don't understand why.

"What else, Clara?" Exhaustion lines his voice, despite being completely unaware of my inner turmoil.

"I got the candles and hemlock. The book was in Latin, though."

"And we both know you're shit at Latin," he says with a chuckle, and I scowl as best I can.

"I may have cussed at it to translate, and it just...did. After I said the incantation, nothing happened. Then the cat showed up and tried to eat the hemlock, so I went to grab him and tumbled into the circle."

His brows pull low and he shakes his head. "What do you—"

"Actually, the pages turned black." I grit my teeth, holding back the cough. Between my lungs being on fire and the dryness in my throat, it's a losing battle.

"Spellsick," he breathes.

I don't know what he's talking about. The book couldn't make me sick. My father warned me about spellsickness, but it was one of those warnings that didn't hold much weight. It was like the bogeyman or Krampus. They were cautionary tales to teach kids a lesson. I know getting ill from messing up spells used to happen in the old covens centuries ago. I assumed we'd evolved enough not to have to worry about things like that anymore.

My eyes flutter closed as a wave of heat washes over me. Fire burns through my veins and licks at my bones. I have no idea if this is from the spell or the trip through the dimensions. Maybe it's from whatever images are hiding in the corners of my mind.

Omen's lips brush my temple as he whispers, "I'll be right back."

Memories flood back to me. Blackness. Numbness. Omen. There's a flash and the dream plays behind my lids once more. Except it didn't feel like a dream. It felt like a prophecy coming to life. Premonition isn't my strong suit. Some witches have the sight. I'm definitely not one of them. No one seems to have that particular gift anymore.

"Clara? What's wrong?" Omen's voice cuts through the terror gripping me. He presses a cold washcloth to my forehead and I bite back a moan. I didn't realize just how hot I was until now.

"I...I saw something," I croak. "When you were bringing me here, I saw something. I don't think I'm spellsick. I'm just... scared." I whisper the last word as if I'll be able to hide from the reality of what I saw.

"What did you see?" he growls.

"Nothing," I breathe.

His hand slides into my hair, and he tips my face up. I meet his gaze and a tear slips down my cheek. The concern in his dark eyes overwhelms me. Twin flames erupt in their depths and the thread tying us together pulls taut. One tug and it'll snap, unleashing everything I've been holding back.

His gaze softens. "What did you see?"

"I saw you dying."

"How exactly did I die?" When I shake my head, he climbs next to me and gathers me in his arms. The washcloth ends up on the floor, and he tucks my head under his chin. "I promise I won't leave after you tell me."

I pull his scent into me, letting the subtle notes soothe my inner jagged edges. I've spent so many years on the fringes of things—my community, my friend group, my family—and I'm sick of it. Being part of something more was never available to me. I tried, really tried, but I could never seem to break through. With Omen, I never feel the need to be anything other than me. And now I have to trust him, even if this is temporary. Even if the premonition is nothing more than my worst fears manifesting themselves.

I pull in a deep breath and describe what I watched in the void between worlds. With my body pressed against his, my muscles relax and the ache once battering me eases a little. Still, the pain of his death remains. I can almost smell the burning of his flesh, the sound of his screams, the bone-deep pain of losing him. I know without a doubt his death will break me. Which seems ridiculous. We're not a couple. We're not lovers, even though we've slept together. We're still trying to navigate this weird dynamic.

I'm a witch. He's a demon. There's no way for us to be anything other than what we are.

His chest vibrates under me, his shoulders shaking and I cling to him. He gasps and I squeeze my eyes shut to stem the flow of my tears. When his fingers dig into my skin, I brace myself for him to move me. Hopefully, he'll take me seriously. I may not have the gift of premonition, but the spell revealed more than I was prepared for. If he thinks I'm exaggerating, he'll send me back and I won't know what to do with myself. The not knowing would plague me for eternity.

"Clara," he wheezes, and a chuckle escapes. "You didn't see me dying."

I try to shove away from him, and he tightens his hold on me. "Let me go, Omen."

"Stop," he growls, the word tumbling around us, and I freeze. He tips my chin up. "Was I smiling? In your dream, premonition, whatever, was I grinning like a damned fool?" I nod and he smirks. "Yeah, you were seeing me in the gauntlet. It's an obstacle course."

"I know what a gauntlet is," I snap as annoyance and humiliation hits me.

"We use it to train the newer demons. I was helping out, showing them how to do it. Except Triton, the trainer, thought it'd be funny to add in something he saw somewhere. I didn't know I'd have to deal with fire lassoing me around the ankle."

I bite my lip, searching his gaze for the lie. It's not there, just mirth. "It's from a movie."

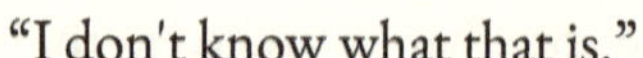

"I don't know what that is."

I sigh, exhaustion swamping me. "You really need to get out more."

"This might be a silly question, but do you feel better?"

"Emotionally, maybe. Physically, not at all."

"Spellsick. Get some sleep and I'll figure something out."

I hum as my lids grow heavy. It'll take more than a simple explanation to get over the thought of Omen dying. I still don't think I'm spellsick, but whatever. He'll do whatever he thinks is necessary regardless of what I think. Which is probably a good thing since I can't think straight. I'll be better when I wake up, as long as he's here.

CHAPTER TWENTY
OMEN

I stalk through the halls, half my mind still with Clara tucked away in my room. Dimitri appears next to me and nods, then grabs me and yanks me through a random door.

"We've gotta stop meeting like this," Dimitri says with a grin that doesn't quite reach his eyes.

"Get to the point, Dimitri."

"You think they actually use any of these cleaning supplies? I mean, it's not like Thursdays are for deep cleaning."

"We don't even have Thursdays in Hell," I grumble.

He tilts his head, contemplating that. "Suppose so. Anyway, what exactly did you do with her after I poofed?"

"I took care of her."

"Well, that isn't ominous," he mutters.

The last thing I want is to give him details about Clara. Not only is it not my story to tell, but it puts her in more danger if he knows. All it would take is a suspicion from one of the upper level demons and they'd be dragging Dimitri's ass into a room. They'd force him to talk, whether he wanted to or not. I won't put him in that position. While Hell works like a well-oiled machine, we're still demons. He'd be tortured for the information in his head.

"You figure out where you're getting summoned to?" I ask. He wrinkles his nose and glances away. "Are you glowing?"

His gaze snaps back to mine. "What? No. Why the fuck would I be glowing? It's not like anything happened to make me light up. I haven't been anywhere. I mean, other than the closet in some random witch's house. At least, I assume they're a witch. I mean, what else could it be?"

"What the fuck is wrong with you?"

"Who, me? Nothing. I told you it's nothing."

The muscle under his eye twitches and he is glowing a deep purple. I don't know if he's on the edge of burnout like I was. While I burst into flames and burn from the inside out, he lights up like a lightning storm. It's just as deadly. This isn't anything like what he usually goes through.

"Holy shit, did you get cursed?"

"What? No." He forces out a laugh.

"Then why's your voice all squeaky and high?" I grip the back of my neck. "First Clara, now you. I just can't catch a fucking break."

"Wait, Clara's cursed too?" He grimaces when I give him a look. "Fine, I *might* be. What's wrong with Clara? Is she still here?"

"I'm not telling you shit. It'll only get both of us in trouble."

Dimitri taps his finger to his chin, then nods. "Fine, but you know you're going to need my help. Especially if she's cursed."

"She's not cursed. She's spellsick." The words slip out before I can stop them.

His face lights up like I've handed him fries. "Omen, seriously? You know what to do. She's spellsick and you're her soulbound. Do the freaky and she'll be better."

I scrub my hands down my face and mumble, "You did not just call it the freaky."

"Oh ho, I did. How you think she got spellsick?"

"She's got a book."

"A grimoire?"

I shake my head. "Not exactly. I've got an idea where it came from, but that shit is sentient. The fucking thing keeps fucking with reality."

"Yet it got you and her together."

"Won't mean shit if the book keeps showing her spells to make her sick."

He rolls his eyes. "Already told you how to help with that. Now, go get your girl." He pushes me around and slaps my ass before shoving me out the door.

Unfortunately, he shoves me straight into Ludovic. The older demon stumbles back. Before I can react, his fist slams into my cheek. Dimitri whispers a curse from behind me. Ludo pulls his fist back again and I raise my arm to block it. He drops his hand to his side.

"Where the fuck have you been?"

Dimitri slides around me, a placating grin on his face. "Ludo! Just the demon I wanted to see. We've got a problem with the gauntlet. Triton says the fireballs keep going haywire. Omen's going to help us out. Hope you don't mind. You can talk to Triton if you do. I'm sure he'll tell you to fuck off, but you can try."

Dimitri claps him on the back, then grabs my arm and hauls me away. He marches us down the hallway, back toward my rooms. Once we're far enough away, he pulls me to a stop.

"You'd better rank up if you don't want Ludo on your ass."

"I'm not ranking up. I like where I am," I grumble.

"Yeah, sure. You just *love* the paperwork and the shit Ludo throws at us, and the portal duties, and the night watches, and—"

"Okay, I get it. I hate my job. Except if I level up, I'll be..." *Alone.*

I'll be completely alone. Except I won't be, not if I keep Clara with me. If she wants to stay here, I could rank up and spend the extra time with her. A new rank would allow me to pick what I want to do, whether it was train new demons or manage the lower ranks. Hell, I could even take over Ludo's job. He'd fucking hate that.

"You know...if you level up, you'd outrank Ludo. Definite perk."

"And I wouldn't be able to go back to the human dimension," I whisper.

"Yeah, but she's here now. Maybe—"

"I'm not having this conversation," I growl.

He nods, then curls his hands into fists as a tremor rocks him. "You should definitely have it with your witch."

"No. I'm not having this conversation at all. I'm not ranking up. I'm not trapping her here. I'm not keeping her."

I stalk off, not waiting for his response. He'll just lecture me some more and try to get me to change my mind. It's hard enough being in this position. Two impossible options. Either I keep things the way they are, hoping the answer drops in my lap, or I resign myself to an eternity of yearning for an existence I'll never experience.

"You can't make decisions for her," Dimitri calls after me. "You don't get to dictate her future, Omen."

I wave without looking, then disappear into the ether. Dimitri isn't wrong. I'm not about to admit that, though. I'm used to making decisions alone and having others follow them. Taking Clara into account, especially when I'm not entirely sure what she'll say, terrifies me.

If I ask her to leave her life behind in the human dimension and stay here, she could end up resenting me. If I follow her home, I'll lose my magic, eventually leaving me a creature born from nightmares. I won't be able to glamour or control my shadows. She'll have to kill me once I no longer recognize her face. I don't want her to go through that. My memories, my friend's remembrance of me, my ability to jump between dimensions. I don't want to lose any of it.

None of it really matters if I lose her, though. Being soulbound means I'll constantly be searching for her. For the rest of my existence, I'll never be free of her memory. Especially now that I know her intimately.

When I step from the void, and land right outside my bedroom door, I let out a sigh of relief. My muscles relax as I enter, anticipating seeing Clara again. I freeze in the doorway and my gaze skips around the space. It's empty, devoid of life, but her scent remains. If she's delirious, she could be wandering around Hell. She could fall into a portal and end up anywhere.

I rush to the bathroom, then back to the bedroom. Living room, office, weapons room, and finally the kitchen. All of them empty. I close my eyes and focus on the thread tying us together. My fist slams into the wall when it doesn't work. I shouldn't be surprised. Trying to use a mythical power I don't know much about is ludicrous.

"Why are you punching things? Also, you lied to me." Clara drops a paper bag on the island made of obsidian like every-thing else in this place. She starts pulling ingredients from inside.

Magic swirls around me and my wings burst from my back. "Where were you?"

She frowns at the ingredients, then shrugs. "I'm not entirely sure. I woke up and you were gone." Her head pops up and she glares at me. "That's what you lied about, if you were wondering. Anyways, I went looking for you. Opened a door and it was an empty closet with this bag and your cat sitting on the floor. You shouldn't lock your cat in a closet, by the way. It's rude."

"You weren't here. I searched the entire house."

"Are you calling me a liar?"

I throw my hands up and stalk around the island. I grab her and haul her into me. She lets out an *oh*. I bury my face in her hair and breathe her in.

"Are you feeling better?"

She shivers and her nails dig into my back. "It comes and goes. I'll be fine."

I cup her cheeks and tip her face up. "I still think you're spellsick."

She gives me a look, pressing her lips together. "Then how do

I get over it? I assume that's what you were doing—trying to figure out how to heal me."

Shit. I can't tell her what Dimitri said. She'll think I'm just trying to fuck her. I am, but that's not the point. Instead of answering, I cover her mouth with mine. She melts into me, parting her lips. I only meant to distract her, yet I'm drawn into her. I should let go, send her home, and leave her be. Except I can't.

She pulls back and whispers, "Omen, we need to talk."

I groan, resting my forehead on hers. "I know."

"If you fuck me, are you going to disappear again?"

I let out a chuckle. "You're here so you wouldn't be summoning me. And I can't be summoned in Hell."

"You can't?"

"Nope. If I was lower rank, sure. It's annoying as shit." I brush my lips over hers. "Are you going to keep asking me questions, or can I fuck you now?"

"I suppose we can discuss the other things later," she murmurs. "Don't think I forgot what you said when you were in that cage. But, yeah, later."

"Perfect."

I wrap my hands around her thighs and carry her toward the bedroom. I could put her on the counter, finish what we started in her own kitchen, but I need her in my bed. If she doesn't stay, at least I'll have the memories. Her scent might fade and her aura will vanish, but I'll remember.

As I lay her down, she clings to me and I have to peel her fingers from my arms. I hook my thumbs in her waistband and stop.

"Do not stop," she says, picking up her hips.

"First, you need to know that fucking you will cure you. I wasn't going to...I mean, I didn't want to—" I huff. "You needed to know."

"I don't really care whether or not it'll cure me." She sits up

and grabs a fistful of my shirt. "I just want to forget the world exists for a bit. And I want to do that with you."

I don't fully believe her, yet I can't stop myself from capturing her lips. She moans as she inches closer to press her hips to mine. I grind into her as I devour her. Or maybe she's devouring me. Honestly, I'll take whatever I can get. Being with her has woken me up in a way I never thought possible.

She rips her mouth away and gasps for air. "Magic."

I lean forward only to jolt back again. "What?"

Her black pupils bleed out, overtaking the bright blue of her irises. "The debt. Spellsick. Time."

"Clara?" I grab her face and brush my thumbs over her cheekbones. "Come back to me."

She blinks, revealing her bright blue eyes once more. "I'm here. I just...the book. I think I'm spellsick because of the book."

I shake my head, but don't dispute her claim. The thing is probably just a conduit, not the actual cause. Could her malevolent spellbook actually be at fault? Maybe. It's more likely because of her transition to Hell. It might be because I refuse to tell her about being soulbound to one another. Whichever it is, she'll continue to get sick until she's in agony. I can't let that happen.

"Clara..."

"It's fine. You said it'd be fine. I just...I figured it out."

I'm caught in the radiance of her smile. It's captivating and I realize how fucked I truly am. She wraps her fingers around my wrists and tugs me closer. I can't resist her, especially when she seals her lips to mine. I fall into her kiss as my shadows swirl around us. All my doubts fade into the background in the wake of my desire for her.

I will my shadows into claws and swipe at her clothing. Before long, the fabric falls away, revealing her smooth skin. My own clothes end up vanishing and she gasps into my mouth. I should slow down, ease her into this and give her time to change her mind. My magic has a mind of its own, though. My shadows are everywhere—digging into her flesh, playing with her nipples, and delving between her legs.

She whimpers, her hips lifting toward me. Her wetness brushes my tip and I groan.

"Easy, little witch," I growl. "I'm barely holding on."

Her nails dig into the back of my neck, and she snarls, "Let go."

It's all the permission I need and I plunge into her. Her head tips back, back arching, a cry on her lips. I hesitate when I'm deep inside her to give her time to adjust. She whines, desperately trying to force me to move. I'm still riding the edge, yet I find the strength to wait.

A chuckle leaves me and her eyes fly open. "Need something, Clara?" I brush my lips over hers and her teeth snap together, barely missing my flesh.

"You're killing me, Omen."

"Killing you? No," I murmur. "I'm saving you."

I pull out, leaving just the tip in her, then thrust again. I repeat the move, slower each time, though it's driving me as feral as it is her. Eventually, my control will snap, but not yet. She gasps with every move, then shudders as I grind into her, making sure she feels all my piercings.

When I pull out completely, a strangled cry leaves her. She sputters out some choice words that would make a lesser demon blush.

"And you say I have a dirty mouth," I mutter, then flip her onto her stomach. She mumbles something into the pillow, cussing or begging, it doesn't really matter.

I grip her hips and pull her onto her knees. Tendrils of my shadows steal across her body and delve between her legs. The longer I'm in Hell, the stronger my magic becomes. With the heightened sensations, I feel every stroke, every shudder, every pulse deep within me.

Clara mumbles something, then pops her head to the side and gasps, "More."

A low growl leaves me and I plunge into her. Both my shadows and my cock fill her up and I groan. The sound mingles with her moans, driving me on. With each thrust, she squeezes around my shaft, bringing me closer to the edge. She pushes back every time I surge into her.

Fire ignites within me and flames engulf my arms, then ripple to my fingers. Clara spasms when the blaze reaches her flesh. They flicker from yellow to orange to blue. A brilliant blue I've seen reflected in her eyes. I dig my fingers into her flesh, then pull out once more.

She slams her hand onto the bed. "What in the actual—"

I flip her around again, and she glares up at me. "I need to watch you come."

Her mouth parts as she blinks up at me. I cover her body with my own and bury my cock into her once more. A soft *oh* falls from her lips and I capture the sound. The thread between us tightens with each thrust.

My magic spins out of control, shadows whipping around us and creating a firestorm overhead. Sparks fall from the dense clouds and sizzle as they hit my skin. When they land on Clara, they flare a bright blue—tiny flames flickering across her flesh.

Her hand slips between us, and I push to my knees. Between her moaning my name, her fingers circling her clit, and my cock disappearing into her, I'm close to losing it. She spasms around my length, sending me hurtling into oblivion. Her cries echo around us and I shudder out my release.

I collapse onto her, careful to keep my weight from crushing her. She wraps her arms around my shoulders and tucks her head into my neck. I flip to my back, taking her with me. She settles on my chest, then spasms around my cock, still buried deep in her. It wouldn't take much for me to recover and take her all over again.

She yawns, grinding any thoughts of round two to a halt. I may not know a lot about being spellsick, but I do know she needs rest. As her breathing evens out, I kiss the top of her head.

She mumbles something in her sleep and I tighten my hold on her.

I realize this might be the last time she'll be in my arms. If things go the way I expect they will, she'll go home soon and I'll have to adjust my existence once more. I'll never revert to who I was before I met her. I wouldn't want to. I shove the thoughts away, unwilling to sully the last few moments I have with her.

CHAPTER TWENTY-ONE
CLARA

I probably should have woken Omen before I slipped out of bed. He was sleeping peacefully and I didn't have the heart to wake him. Plus, he deserves it for leaving me while I was sick. It's not like I'm going far. Hopefully, he doesn't freak out and punch a wall again.

"Hey, Kitty Cat," I coo as I step into the kitchen. He meows and I scratch him under the chin. "Are you supposed to be on the counter or is Omen going to threaten to skin you if he catches you?"

His tail pops up and he stretches before jumping down. I smile as he sashays away. I still need to ask Omen what the cat's actual name is. It almost feels like it's been too long, though. He hasn't corrected me so far, but I doubt he calls the cat Handsome or Kitty Cat. Sunshine is definitely out since he's not orange. Plus, his behavior doesn't lend to a sunny disposition. Omen probably calls him something ridiculous like Bane or Charcoal.

I set about gathering all the ingredients for cinnamon bread. Part of me wonders if I should question a bag full of baking supplies found in a closet. Then again, Omen didn't say anything and this is his place. Maybe Hell often leaves groceries out based on cravings. Who am I to question these things?

I search around for music, but the kitchen is devoid of literally anything. As I go through the cupboards, I wonder if I'll even

find a bread pan to bake this thing in. I open a drawer and go back to the cupboards on the bottom.

"What the fuck," I mutter. "How much magic is in this place? Random cooking utensils shouldn't just pop up."

Once I've found everything, I set about mixing the ingredients. The kitchen could probably provide me with a mixer, but I need to do something with my hands. It's not until I'm halfway through I realize I don't have any eggs. I glance around the space as if they'll magically appear. If Hell can bring me all the supplies and tools, it can get me some fucking eggs.

Omen stumbles into the kitchen, sweatpants hung low on his hips. My mouth waters as I stare at his crotch. He clears his throat and my eyes pop up.

"My eyes are up here, little witch. What are you making?"

"Uh, bread?"

"That a question?" He leans against the counter and peeks in the bowl.

"No. It's bread. Cinnamon bread. I need eggs, though. Do you have any?"

He shakes his head. "Nope. I don't keep food here. I eat in the mess or with Dimitri. He cooks, but food down here is different. You need eggs, though, I'll get you eggs."

He disappears before I can question him about how food is different. I never thought about how demons eat. In my mind, the fries were a fluke. Omen has a weird amalgamation of knowledge when it comes to the human realm. I scoot around the counter and haul myself up on a tall stool. My feet dangle and I kick them back and forth. If he takes forever, I'm going to end up getting bored.

"Got it," he calls in triumph ten seconds before he appears.

"That is not an egg," I choke out.

"Yes, it is." He turns the thing over in his hands.

"Well, maybe, but I need a chicken egg. Those don't have scales and they certainly aren't iridescent. Oh and that thing is about fifty times bigger than a chicken egg."

He scowls at the thing, then bellows, "Dimitri."

The other demon pops in before Omen's voice fades and I jolt. At least I don't scream this time.

"Hey, Clara. Nice to see you're still in Hell." Dimitri flashes me a grin before turning to Omen. "Uh, why do you have a dragon egg? And how the fuck did you get it away from the horde?"

"It was just sitting there in the coals. I just grabbed it. She needs eggs. Not this egg. Like, squawking eggs."

"Chicken," I say, fighting a grin.

"I know, but they squawk. Funny little fuckers."

"Perhaps you should take the dragons back their egg. I'll keep Clara company."

"The fuck you will. Get your own witch," Omen snarls and shoves the dragon egg into Dimitri's chest. "Take this back and get us the right egg."

Dimitri opens his mouth to argue and I clear my throat. "Please and thank you, Dimitri."

His eyes narrow and I swear smoke swirls in them. "Fine. But I'm doing this for *you* because you're actually nice to me. And you have manners."

He snatches up the egg and vanishes. Thunder rumbles overhead and I glance up. The ceiling flashes, revealing dark swirling clouds overhead. In a blink, it's back to normal, though what's normal, I don't know. I feel like I should know more about this place. My mother probably has some books about it I tucked away in my spell room. They were written by witches, though, so I don't know how accurate they'd be.

"We should actually talk now, shouldn't we?" I whisper.

"Suppose we should. What did you want to talk about?"

"Well, my spellsickness, which I'm still not convinced that's what it was, is gone. You didn't die a horrific death at the bottom of a chasm. And I'm in Hell after falling into your summoning circle."

"None of those are things we need to actually talk about.

We've settled all of those...issues." He settles onto the stool next to me and sighs. "You can't stay in Hell, Clara."

I nod, hiding the stab of pain his announcement brings. "I figured. Witches aren't exactly built for all this, huh?"

"Not usually." He drops his elbows on the counter and stares at the bowl.

"What's that mean?"

He shakes his head. "Nothing."

I don't believe him, obviously. Dragging anything out of him seems damn near impossible. Despite that, he usually lets it slip eventually. I don't know how long I can wait for his walls to break down, though. I don't know if I *want* to wait.

Part of me thinks it would be easier to walk away now. Our experiences have been stilted and I'm worried I'm clinging to something I've built up in my mind. Him randomly popping into my life added to the chaos. I thrived off it when it felt like the rest of my life was falling apart.

Yet I can't deny I feel better when I'm around him. I'm happier when he's in front of me. I feel safer when I'm with him. Something is tying us together, shoving us into each other's orbits. A voice screams at me from the ether, telling me to sit up, pay attention, don't let a good thing go. In the time we've spent together, I've seen what my future could be—uncertain and full of hope.

"So, you'll take me back and then what?"

He clears his throat. "Actually—"

"Got it," Dimitri cries as he appears next to me. Omen's hand shoots out and steadies me as I rock back on the stool.

I hop down and grab the eggs from him. "Thanks, Dimitri."

I hurry around the island and crack them into the bowl. Whatever Omen was about to say, I'm not ready for. I just want to make this bread. Omen pulls Dimitri from the room, and I swallow hard as I concentrate on the dough forming in front of me. I spend the next few minutes trying to convince myself I don't want to stay in Hell even if it was an option.

I don't succeed.

As I knead the dough, I focus on the rhythm—push, roll, turn, push, roll, turn. It's enough to center me. By the time Omen steps back into the kitchen, sans his friend, I've got my shit together. He watches me for a minute, then collapses onto the stool.

"How long will the bread take?" he asks softly.

"It's gotta rise for a bit, then it can be baked. You know how to do that?"

He snorts. "I don't even know how to turn the oven on, little witch."

"I can show you." My nose itches and I sniff, hoping he doesn't think I'm about to cry. I am, but that's not the point. I didn't think I'd be heartbroken over leaving Hell—over leaving him. "Then you can bake it and you'll have fresh bread."

"Or you could just stay and do it. You don't have to leave—"

"If I do it for you, you'll never learn."

"And if you keep interrupting me, we'll never have a full conversation." He shoves to his feet. "I'm going to take a shower."

He stalks from the room, his shadows trailing him. As soon as I finish this, I'm going to ask him to take me back. Rip off the Band-Aid and all that. No use hanging around when he's so conflicted over my presence. I should tell him I want to stay, though.

I scrunch my nose over and over as the itch intensifies. With my fingers full of dough, I resort to using my sleeve, but it doesn't help. I end up shaking my hands and my head, desperately trying to get it to stop.

Omen's cat curls his way around my legs, and I glance down. "You got claws, Handsome? Because I could definitely use them right now."

I glance up and to the right. I think I heard it's supposed to stop the itching. Or maybe that's sneezing. Doesn't matter, since it doesn't work.

The cat hisses, then flounces away. "Omen would have helped me, ungrateful little brat."

I tip my head back and close my eyes. I probably look ridiculous, wiggling my entire face.

"What's wrong?" Omen says from directly behind me.

"My nose itches," I whine.

He chuckles and presses his chest into my back. Sweet relief hits me as he scratches my nose. It's not until I open my eyes, I realize he's using his shadows. A shiver runs through my body, though whether it's from his closeness or the reprieve, I don't know. He drops his hand to my hip and slips the other around my waist. I rest my head on his chest, and he presses a kiss to my temple.

"What are we going to do?" I whisper.

He sighs and holds me closer. "I can't guarantee time will be on our side. If I keep going back and forth, it might be longer. We could go years without seeing each other. You don't deserve to have your existence put on hold waiting around for me."

"Except my only other option is Brandon."

He tenses, a rumble rattling in his chest. "Don't say his name."

"What happens to witches who stay in Hell? Do they die? Am I technically dead right now?"

"Clara, you're not a ghost or dead. It's just another dimension. Yes, some souls come down here when they die, but witches go to another dimension usually. You're just...here."

We need to keep having this conversation, but I don't want to do it with my hands full of dough. "I need you to move."

He drops his hold on me and steps away. I glance over my shoulder at him, then scan the area.

"Uh, where's the sink? I need to wash my hands. And I'll need cling wrap or a towel for this."

He snaps his fingers and a sink appears. Another snap and a towel flutters in front of me and settles on the bowl. There are so many things I don't understand when it comes to Omen and

Hell. I just went along with whatever was happening. I trusted karma or fate or the forces of the dimensions to guide me. Now, it feels like I'm making a series of missteps. Too scared to tell him what I want. Too annoyed to call him on his bullshit. Too tired to question anything.

As the warm water rushes over my hands, I attempt to imagine my life with him—and without him. Do I take the leap and hope he wants to stay with me? Do I cut my losses and live a life of solitude? Or do I spend the rest of my time waiting for him to show up?

My spine snaps straight and I spin around. "I don't think we should keep going like we are."

He nods, avoiding my gaze. I open my mouth to explain when he finally lifts his head. Sorrow rests in the blackness, and a familiar ache takes up residence in my heart.

"It's been a pleasure, little witch."

He snaps his fingers and the world goes dark.

CHAPTER TWENTY-TWO
OMEN

Raw anguish rips through me, rendering me useless. My shadows abandon me and leave another hole in my soul next to the gaping one Clara left behind. I gasp for air, yet my lungs refuse to work.

It's an apt punishment for what I've done. Karma was kind enough to remind me when they dropped by. Dimitri wasn't much better. He raged at me for sending her back without a proper conversation. He wasn't there, though.

He didn't see the fear and regret swimming in her eyes. She didn't want to stay in Hell. She didn't want to stay with me. Offering her the option at that point would only make things awkward.

If she wanted to still see me, she would have summoned me. Yet the familiar tug has been absent these last six weeks. I don't blame her. We've had a tumultuous relationship. I wasn't very welcoming at first. She was kind, and I repaid that kindness with sarcasm and insults. Once I let her in, things may have gotten better. It wasn't enough.

Once I catch my breath, I stare at the dark ceiling. Ever-present dark clouds swirl above me. My entire place has been overrun with shadows and darkness. I'm sure it's merely picking up on my own emotions. Doesn't mean it isn't annoying. They aren't very good company. Not like my own shadows, which have abandoned me since Clara left. Since I sent her home.

"Get up," Dimitri barks from the doorway and I roll my head around. "Ludovic wants to see you."

I wave my hand and go back to watching the patterns forming above me. "Tell him I'll find him later."

"No. Now. You've been wallowing for weeks now. He wants you back at work."

"Tell him to demote me, then."

He prowls closer, his lip curling at the state of my room. "You'll lose your powers. Just like you lost her."

"I didn't lose her. I let her go so she'd be free to live her life." I scowl when he yanks the comforter off me. "You'd do well to let me live mine."

He crosses his arms. "Get up or I'm calling Providence."

"My sister won't come. We're not exactly a family of interventionists. She'll let me waste away as I see fit. I'm content where I am."

"Well, I already talked to her, and she said if you don't do something about your issue, she'll be paying your little witch a visit."

My body rockets upright and fire dances along my arms. "Leave Clara alone."

He gives me a look of disgust. "When was the last time you showered? Your horns are molting and your hair is greasy as shit. I swear to fuck, you need to get your shit together before you actually do waste away."

"I'm serious, Dimitri. No one goes topside. No one bothers her. She's living the life Fate laid out for her. She doesn't need more demons popping into her life. You saw how well that worked the last time."

He holds his hands up in surrender. "I'm not the one you should be worried about."

"Fuck," I breathe and jump from my bed.

He steps in front of me, blocking my way. "You might want

pants. Nothing like showing up to a witch's house with your cock hanging out."

I glance down, then scowl as I stomp toward the bathroom. "Wouldn't be the first time."

"What was that?" he calls after me.

"Fuck off," I yell, slamming the door.

The last thing I need is him breathing down my neck, analyzing my every move. As much as I want to immediately jump through dimensions and intercept Prov, I also don't think she'd listen to me if I look like I'm falling apart at the seams. My sister will listen to me if I show her I'm fine.

"How long do I have?" I bellow.

"Don't know. Better hurry."

I take the fastest shower ever, wishing I had enough magic to skip this part. I tug on a pair of jeans and grab a shirt. Skipping through dimensions might land me flat on my ass. I'm loath to admit I need Dimitri's help. When I open the door, he's busy cleaning up my room. Shame hits me square in the chest and I clear my throat.

"You don't have to—"

"We're not talking about it. You ready? Providence is probably already on her way, if you're going to try to intercept her so you can avoid the inevitable." He waves me toward him, then laces our fingers together.

"You know we don't have to hold hands, right?"

"A little moral support never hurt anyone." He gives me a halfhearted smile, then whisks us away.

It takes longer than usual to muck our way through the void. I'm forced to relive my time with Clara. It's painful, yet cathartic. I see her every time I fall asleep, which is why I spend so much time in bed. If I can't be with her physically, then I'll be with her in my dreams.

The longer I'm away from her, the harder it is to stop myself from going topside. I'd gladly make a fool of myself, begging and pleading for her to give us a chance. All the reasons I had for not

offering her to bind herself to me mean nothing. I should have told her we were soulbound.

As soon as we emerge on Clara's street, I've made my decision. If she's happy, content, and living her life, then I'll leave her be. If she's not, I'll convince her to come back to Hell with me. It's the only way I'll be able to move on.

"Listen, when we get in there, don't be weird," Dimitri mutters as we make our way down the dusty lane.

"I don't know what that means."

"Just don't start blubbering or something. Witches don't like that. A couple tears when the situation dictates, okay. Full on sobbing when no one died? Awkward. Especially with your sister there. She'll demote you for that alone."

"We're the same rank. She can't demote me, first of all. Second, I'm not going to blubber. I'm perfectly fine. As long as Providence hasn't messed with her mind, we'll be fine." I pick up my pace, forcing Dimitri to stumble in my wake.

As her house comes into view, I slow down. "Maybe you should stay here. Just wait for Providence to show up."

"What? You don't want me there for your reunion?"

I walk away without answering. I don't have to talk to Clara, though I have a feeling I won't be able to resist if I see her. Her house remains vine free so I doubt it's been too long. Unless she moved. Or hired someone to deal with them. Or maybe it's been a hundred years and she's...no. That doesn't make sense. Time may move differently, but not *that* differently.

I peek in the front window, trying to catch a glimpse of her. My heart hammers in my chest when she comes into view. She looks...good. Frazzled, but good. With her dark hair in a messy bun and a flush on her cheeks, she takes my breath away. I swallow hard, at war with myself on whether to knock.

Clara blows a strand of hair from her face and stomps out of view. Providence hasn't shown up, and Clara seems fine. I should walk away—go back to Hell and deal with my slowly imploding existence. I should rank up and remove the temptation of coming

back here. I should do a lot of things, yet my feet are rooted to the ground. One more glimpse of her is all I need.

"Omen, stop," Dimitri hisses from behind me and I glance over my shoulder. He waves his hand frantically, and I huff before making my way back to him.

I'm only halfway when relief washes over me at the familiar tug in my gut. My face splits into a grin as I vanish, then reappear in Clara's bedroom. Her scent hits me hard and emotions tumble through me, threatening to bring me to my knees. A string of muttered curses floats from the attached bathroom, and I shuffle to the side.

She's hunched over the toilet, her shoulders jerking up and down. I have no idea what she's doing, but I don't think she's hurt. We've had enough of that to last us a lifetime. She pauses, wheezing as she straightens and tips her head back.

"This never would have happened in Hell," she mutters. "Magic would have magically taken care of it."

I smirk at her statement, then sober, clearing my throat.

She doesn't squeal or startle, merely huffs in response. "You've got to be fucking kidding me."

She turns slowly and we stare at each other. I drink her in, searching for any changes. Nothing. She looks exactly like she did the last time I saw her. I don't know what I expected, but it's both comforting and unnerving. Asking her how long it's been on this plane seems ill-advised. Especially since she's glaring at me.

"Hello, little witch."

"Hello? That's all you got?" she growls. "You teleport my ass out of Hell without so much as a conversation, then show up with just a simple hello? Fuck you, Omen."

She spins around and continues messing with the toilet. I want to ask her how long it's been, how she is, if she's missed me. Instead, my mind goes blank.

"What are you doing?"

"Plunging the toilet. Your fucking cat knocked an entire roll of toilet paper in and I didn't notice. Half the thing dissolved and

got stuck." She whips around and shoves a finger at me. "And don't even tell me I should have fished it out. I did and it still plugged up. So, unless you're here to take over, I don't need any tips or pointers or advice or whatever else you're selling."

I hum as she spins around. I could leave her to it or...I grab her around the waist and lift her. She does squeal this time and my palms tingle. I set her in the shower.

"What am I doing here?" I ask as I gaze at the stick poking from the bowl.

"I have no idea what the hell you're doing, Omen," she shrieks. She shoves the glass door open as if she'll climb out.

"I'm fixing your toilet, but I don't know what plunging is."

A hysterical laugh leaves her, and she stops fighting with the door. "There's a suction cup at the bottom of the handle. You put it over the hole and push it up and down. A lot. And you might get toilet water on yourself. It might leak or splash out of the bowl. In fact, it's almost impossible not to. So why don't you just...go back to Hell and let me deal with this."

I glance at her and raise an eyebrow. "I thought you said to take over? That's what I'm doing."

"I don't need your help," she snarls.

"Yet here I am," I murmur, then get to work.

It's not easy, especially with Clara trying to clamber from the shower every thirty seconds. My shadows decide to make an unexpected appearance, and they hold her in place. She yelps and I smirk as I start plunging. It isn't easy with the suction part slipping every few seconds. Plus, it keeps getting stuck in a weird position. The damn cup keeps flipping in on itself.

"Why don't you just do that weird snapping thing," she asks, irritation lining her voice.

"Magic's been wonky," I mutter as I focus on not spilling the water over the lip.

"All magic or just yours?" she asks softly.

I grit my teeth. "Just mine."

"Is that why you didn't leave when I told you to go back to Hell?"

"Probably. Either way, doesn't matter."

A prickle of sensation trickles from my shadows, and I breathe a sigh of relief. Before, I didn't care about their absence. At least not enough to actively worry about it. They were gone and there was nothing I could do about it. I assumed it was my punishment for being with Clara, even if for a short time. I accepted it willingly. In the back of my mind, though, I agonized over whether they'd pop up again or if I'd lost them forever.

"Is that because of me?" she whispers.

"No. It's because of me."

CHAPTER TWENTY-THREE
CLARA

I want to ask him what happened, but the words stick in my throat. Despite his declaration, I know his magic issues are my fault. If I would've stayed away from the book, none of this would be happening. Omen's paying for my decisions. I need to tell him, but from the look on his face, the revelation wouldn't go down well. He's already pissed and I'm not about to make it worse.

I don't know how to act around him anymore. Lashing out and arguing with him is justified. Him showing up without a warning after a month isn't something I had on my to-do list today. Plunging the toilet wasn't either.

When he sent me back here, I thought I'd never see him again. I'd love to say I've been perfectly fine when, in fact, I've been wallowing. When Omen's cat showed up, I raged. I ended up throwing a strawberry at him, then a carrot when he didn't move. I missed him both times, then broke down crying. It wasn't my finest moment.

It took me a while to pull my shit together, but once I did, Handsome went wild. He got into the cupboards and knocked a couple glasses out. As I was cleaning up the shards of glass, he proceeded to shred my throw pillow. The stuffing ended up everywhere. I swear I'm going to be finding fluff for weeks. I didn't even notice the cat got into the bathroom. Little shithead.

And now I'm here, with a demon in my bathroom, and he's

plunging my toilet. And I don't know how to act or feel. And I'm desperately trying not to jump him or cry. He looks good—better than good. As pissed as I am for him bouncing me back here without a conversation, I'm still captivated by him, which is highly inconvenient. I want to stay mad for a while.

"Are you..." I cross my arms, and a shiver rolls through me as his shadows loop around my throat. It's a light caress, enough to let me know he's there. "Why are you here?"

Water sloshes over the rim of the toilet, yet he doesn't stop plunging. "Providence."

"Um, we talking fate or fortune?"

He pauses and glances at me. "Neither. Providence."

"Um, what?"

He huffs and goes back to plunging. "Providence is my sister."

"You have a sister?" It hits me how much I don't know about him.

He shrugs, making everything worse. "It's not like humans. We don't really have parents or siblings. She just happens to be a mirror of me. It's more...our jobs than anything else. She seems to think she can interfere with my decisions when she thinks I'm fucking up."

I press my lips together. "What'd you fuck up?"

He shakes his head. When he tugs the plunger from the hole, I wince. Water splashes onto his jeans. I want to take the question back. I almost feel like I'm pulling information from him with a crowbar. He leans back and glares at the toilet.

I step from the shower, making sure to not touch him. I grab the handle and push down once. The water bubbles, then gurgles, and begins to drain.

"Well, that's that, I suppose. Thanks," I whisper.

"Are you happy?" he blurts out.

I shrug as I flush the toilet again and breathe a sigh of relief. Now I'll have to clean up the mess in here.

"Can you get the cat to leave my stuff alone? I don't know

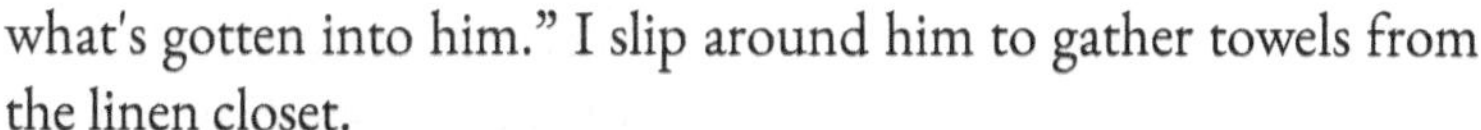

what's gotten into him." I slip around him to gather towels from the linen closet.

"How exactly would I get your cat to do anything?"

I swing around, brandishing the plunger between us. "*My* cat? Oh no. You're not foisting that menace off on me."

"It's not foisting if he belongs to you, Clara."

"He doesn't belong to me," I cry.

"If you don't stop swinging that thing around, I'm going to—"

"To what? Disappear? Newsflash, I'm pretty used to that when it comes to you." I sober and drop my hand to my side. "I'm sorry. That was uncalled for. You don't owe me anything. Thank you for helping me."

"Don't do that," he whispers. "You have every right to be upset with me. I didn't give you any warning before I sent you back. I thought it would be easier that way."

"Was it? For you, I mean. Was it easier that way?"

"No, it wasn't."

"Probably didn't help that your magic wasn't working. Seems to be fine now," I murmur, then sigh. "I know you said it was because of you, but I think it was the book. Or rather, me using the book."

"Worth it," he breathes. At least, that's what I think he said. Omen grips the back of his neck and sighs. A scowl takes over his face, and he stalks past me. Irritation overrides my guilt, and I grit my teeth.

"You know, it's pretty annoying when we're in the middle of a conversation and you just take off. Which is what I was saying before. Seems like I shouldn't have to explain that to you." I shuffle back to the bathroom and toss the plunger inside the shower. I'll deal with it later, once he's left and I need a distraction from the grief.

Omen's hand wraps around my arm and tugs me toward the front door. "We're not done talking, but I have to deal with Dimitri. Also, you're the one who summoned me."

"To open a jar of spaghetti sauce," I cry as I stumble down the stairs. He snatches me around the waist and lifts me clean off my feet.

"I mean today. I was outside because of Providence, but I wasn't going to bother you."

I sputter, not sure how to respond, especially with the distraction. His heat seeps into me, and I don't know what to do with my hands. Serenity steals over me, settling in my bones and lodging into my heart—my soul. A missing piece clicks into place, but I shy away from it.

"So you only came because of another demon? You're not exactly helping your cause here, Omen."

His lips brush the shell of my ear and I shiver. "Bold of you to assume I have a cause, little witch."

"Omen, why are you manhandling a witch?" a deep feminine voice calls out, and my head snaps up.

Omen sets me on my feet, yet keeps his arm around my waist. "Providence, this is Clara. And I wasn't manhandling her. In fact, I was saving her from herself, which is entirely necessary."

"I'm perfectly capable of taking care of myself, thank you very much," I snap.

"Sure you are, little witch."

Providence scans me up and down. She towers over me like Omen and Dimitri. There isn't really a resemblance between Omen and her. Her black skin shimmers as if infused with glitter. Her eyes are completely silver, with a pinprick of gold in the center. Mesmerizing is the only way to describe her.

Providence tilts her head and narrows her eyes. It's highly disconcerting. "A witchy demon, I see."

"I'm sorry, I'm not a demon."

"No, but when you're soulbound to a demon, you take on some of their magic, hence, a witchy demon." She says it so matter-of-factly, as if it's common knowledge.

Omen tightens his hold on me. "Time to go, Providence."

She smirks. "So much for leaving things to chance, hmm?"

Dimitri grabs her wrist and they vanish. I didn't even notice him standing behind her I was so focused on Omen's sister. Her cryptic message doesn't mean anything to me. I have no idea what soulbound is or why it pertains to me. From the look on Omen's face, though, he does. Which means he's been keeping a lot more to himself than I thought.

"Want to explain all that?" I murmur.

He sighs heavily. "Let's go inside. Then you can banish me properly afterward."

He trudges back to the house as I trail behind him. Every time I think we're making some type of progress, he pulls away, or a cat jumps into the mix, or a demon drops a random bombshell, or I get scared.

I'm sick of being scared. I'm sick of living my life afraid of someone else's reaction. I'm sick of pretending I don't deserve more.

My feet stutter to a stop. No more living halfway. I refuse to feel guilty about my feelings.

"No."

Omen freezes, then slowly spins around. "No?"

I tip my chin up. "No. We're having this out right here, right now. No going inside. No banishing or vanishing until we've had a proper conversation. Oh, and if someone else shows up, I'm kicking them in the shins."

His eyebrows rise with each word I say. "Shins? Worried you won't be able to reach their knees?"

"Listen here, bucko. Just because you're demons and I can't get my foot that high doesn't mean you have to point it out."

He tilts his head, eyes narrowing, and I finally see the resemblance to his sister. "Don't love that you called me bucko."

"Well, I don't love that you're keeping shit from me. What's soulbound?"

His throat bobs and he glances away. "Souls have holes in them. Not literally, obviously. They're like..."

"Puzzle pieces?"

"Yes. On their own, they function just fine. They're still a piece, but it doesn't show the entire picture. When souls find the pieces that fit their own, they become whole. They merge seamlessly, creating something new."

"Their magic flows from one to the other," I whisper.

He finally meets my gaze. "If one has magic, yes. I believe humans call it soulmates."

"Humans are more loosey-goosey about it. At least, some of them are."

"Some demons don't believe in soulbounds. There's a skeptic in every group. Keeps us from falling for fools, I suppose."

"And we're—I mean, that's us? Is that why you came when I summoned a demon?"

He shakes his head. "You drew my sigil. Was there some divine force involved? I don't know. They're meddlesome, but also flighty. Might have been that damned book of yours. We could have gone our entire existence without meeting. And we would have been fine."

"Fine, but not content. Fine, but not happy. Not truly."

"It doesn't mean we have to...I didn't want you to find out," he snarls, frustration sending his shadows whirling. Flames burst from his fingertips and lick up his arms.

"So you were never going to say anything. You came here for months, helped me when you didn't need to, you...you *fucked* me. You did all of that without telling me we were soulmates—*soulbound*—and you had no intention of ever saying anything. You were going to disappear and leave me to be incomplete. Do I have that right?"

"I wanted you to choose me," he explodes. "I didn't want to influence you, thinking you were stuck with me. Besides, none of that erases the issue of you being a witch. I can't stay on this plane without losing everything in Hell, including my magic."

I nod, chewing on the inside of my cheek. It's a nervous habit I haven't done in years. While I don't agree with his reasonings, I

can understand them. I also don't have a counterargument. Yet. With the fire blazing over his skin, I have a little time to figure it out.

"You wanted me to choose you, but didn't give me all the information to make an informed decision. Which is moot anyways, because if you wouldn't have sent me back, you would have known I was going to ask if I could stay in Hell." It takes him a few seconds to process what I've said. "You let fear control you. What do you want, Omen?"

His flames wink out, his shadows dissipating until only he remains. Reddish skin glowing in the sunlight. A soft glimmer flickering in his eyes. Dark hair ruffling in the soft breeze. He's infuriating and comforting. He drives me up a wall, yet all I want is him to say he wants me.

"I want you to be happy. Blissfully, deliriously happy. I want you to thrive, no matter where you are. I want you to see your worth—to know that you're enough. I want to know every single version of you. That's what I want."

Tears fill my eyes and I swipe them away as soon as they escape. "Is there a way to put my house in Hell?"

He rocks back on his heels. "I could probably pull some strings."

"You know"—I step closer to him—"I think you deserve happiness, too." I close the gap between us, but he doesn't move to touch me.

"Don't tell anyone, but you make me happy."

"Then I suppose we should try doing this whole happy thing together, shouldn't we?"

"I suppose we should."

His hands slide into my hair and his lips brush mine. I grip his shoulders and press my body closer. He deepens the kiss and I lose myself in him. I don't know what the future brings and it's terrifying. Like taking a leap off a cliff in the dark.

I pull back and he growls. "Will my plants die?"

He chuckles. "They'll be fine. And if they're not, we'll figure it out together."

"Together."

EPILOGUE
CLARA

Six months later in Hell

"Clara," Omen bellows, a warning leeching into his tone.

I wince, shoving the pots of plants deeper into the greenhouse and hiding them among the others. I've barely got the door closed when he prowls into view.

"Hey, babycakes." My voice breaks on the nickname and he scowls. I've been trying to find a nickname for the last six months. He vetoes every single one. I don't blame him. I'm not that type of creative, though I didn't think big demon was bad. It was a nice juxtaposition to his nickname for me. Dimitri ruined it by making it dirty.

"One, no to babycakes. Two, why are demons asking me about their potions? I thought you were only doing plants?"

"Oh, that." I slip past him and make my way toward the house. *My* house, which Omen was able to get zapped into Hell. He didn't even care he was giving up his own quarters, though he did upgrade my oven. I wasn't complaining. Should we be living together after such a disjointed relationship? Who knows, but it's worked so far, so I'm not complaining.

"You can't just walk away and think I'll forget about it, Clara," he calls after me.

I sigh, then face him. "Listen, I was just trying to help Triton.

He needed a little boost of confidence to ask Lark to go see the lava fields. It's not like I was giving him a love potion."

He gives me a look. "Do you even know how to make a love potion?"

"Love potions don't exist. You can't fake love, sweetcheeks."

He stalks closer, a grin on his face. He loops his arm around my waist and hauls me into him. "You certainly can't fake my love."

"Well, not everyone can be as lucky as us in love," I say. "So sweetcheeks is the one?"

His smile drops. "No, little witch. Sweetcheeks is not the one. You'll just have to keep trying, I suppose. Now, where'd you get the recipe for the confidence boost?"

I duck my head and attempt to wiggle my way out of his hold. "Just one I had lying around."

"The fucking book."

"It's fine, Omen. It's basically not even malevolent anymore. It's home in Hell." I peek at him through my lashes. "Just like me."

He sighs, resting his forehead against mine. "Fine, but try not to bind anyone to a dragon."

"No promises."

He growls and throws me over his shoulder. A giggle explodes from me as he rushes for the house. He wanted me to be happy. Blissfully, deliriously happy. Being here, with him, I am. I've actually never been more content in my life. Despite the many conversations and arguments we've had, we're still working through things. Still, I feel like I'm finally at home with him.

Binding myself to him, my soulbound, was the best decision I've ever made. We might bicker more than I expected, but I wouldn't have it any other way. I'm exactly where I'm supposed to be.

Thank you so much for reading Omen and Clara's story!
Ready for another adventure?
Check out the other works available by Emilia Abraham.

If you'd like to hear about the other stories that have been living in
my head, sign up for my newsletter (including extra scenes &
epilogues), visit my website, or follow me on social media visit:
emiliaabraham.com

Special Thanks:

K.B. Barrett Designs-Cover Artist and Formatter
Dragon Smith Publishing, LLC-Emily Michel-Editor
Erenee-Beta Reader
Krysten-Omega Reader

ALSO BY
E. ABRAHAM

Shadows of Synd:

Under the Shadows-Book 1

Between the Shadows: Novella

Running From Shadows-Book 2

Becoming Shadows-Book 3

Shadows Within Us-Book 4

Beyond the Shadows-Book 5

Ruins of Rima: Spin-off Series

Chasing Darkness-Book 1

Charmed by Darkness-Book 2

Havoc in Harris Duology:

Phantom Betrayal

Novella:

Cadence of the Xylophone

Available on Newsletter:

Extra Scenes,

Bridging Epilogues

ALSO BY
EMILIA ABRAHAM

Stuck at Sundown

Write on the Edge

The Cryptid Chronicles:

Bewitched by Bigfoot

Seduced by the Sliver Cat

ABOUT
E. ABRAHAM

After many years of dreaming of becoming a full-time writer, Emilia Abraham took the leap, bringing her words to print. From sweet contemporary romance to spicy why choose and everything in between, she focuses on the happily ever after.

Emilia lives in the Upper Midwest with her husband (who's probably sick of listening to her expound on fictional men) and three kids (who try to steal her post-it notes). When she's not writing, she enjoys reading, playing video games, and consuming copious amounts of energy drinks.